CHRISTMAS NIGHT BEAR: WYATT

SILVERTIP SHIFTERS

J.K. HARPER

CHRISTMAS NIGHT BEAR

Can a wounded, possessive bear and a stubborn, holiday-hating reindeer heal their busted hearts just in time to make some mistletoe magic that will last forever?

A reindeer shifter fleeing her past...
Brynna Darby can't help that she's a reindeer shifter. But she sure can do her darned best to ignore that part of her life, and has done so for years. Until she abruptly lands back in her tiny shifter hometown. Expectations there are suffocating her—but one sexy bear shifter might open up her guarded heart and show her how to find joy again.

A bear shifter searching for home...
Wyatt Webber returned to his hometown of Deep Hollow right before Christmas, his favorite time of year. Then he runs into the onetime love of his life, Brynna, and everything threatens to turn into a lump of coal. She's the mate who broke his heart...but she also might be the only one who can put it back together again.

B rynna Darby flung up her hands in victory and hollered out to the cold December sky, "YASS!"

Whooping with joy, she danced on the cement pathway beside the railing decorated with shiny garlands of red and green in honor of the holidays. She didn't care one little bit about looking like a total goof in front of others who also traveled the frozen Silvertip Creek walkway. She was a freaking champion runner, woot!

Just moments ago, that final daunting hill had appeared ahead of her, right at the point when her leg muscles usually started to scream in protest. But she'd gritted her teeth, dug in, and pushed her way up the short but steep hill. Passing her trainer in a burst of speed, huffing out a single shout of laughter as he muttered something about dirty pool, she'd raced up that hill on two legs that today felt as strong and solid as they'd ever been.

She was just about healed up from her injury. That meant she was *thisclose* to being able to escape her hometown once more. This time, she would never look back.

A quiet grumble very deep inside her floated up, but Brynna ignored it. No. Deep Hollow was her past, and she wanted no part of it anymore.

With a somewhat theatrical groan, Thor, her sister's fiancé and also Brynna's physical therapist and training partner, reached her side. "Way to hand a guy his balls," he complained cheerfully if also slightly breathlessly. "Good job, Bryn."

He smiled down at her with the genuine pride of a trainer who had done his job well, then gave her a brotherly ruffle on her head. "You owned this run. Just like you owned the last several runs. So," he drawled out with a big grin, "I think we're gonna have to declare you officially fit and ready to go back to work, little deer."

Breath catching in her throat, Brynna ignored the irritating nickname as she stared up at him.

"Shut up," she said in a near whisper. "For real? You're going to declare me fully healed?"

Thor nodded. "You just ran like you were on fire and beat the hell out of me. For the third time this week, no less. My official word is that you're healed, sister-to-be," he said in a gentle but firm voice. "For real."

With another happy shriek, Brynna leaped forward to give him a quick hug before whirling away to dance an even more excited jig on the pathway, scattered snow crunching underfoot. This time she got more stares and a few giggles from passersby, but they all still seemed cheerful. This time of year did that to people.

She felt utterly giddy with happiness. She was whole, she was healed, and most importantly, now she'd be able to get the hell out of tiny shifter town Deep Hollow, Colorado, a.k.a. the bane of her existence. Just being here, trapped at her parents' house for the past six weeks while she recuperated from a bad tibial fracture caused by that distracted teenager driving his scooter like a madman through Rome, had been making her go mad.

Just holiday nerves, the little voice in her mind whispered in a comforting tone. *Reindeer don't go mad. They just sometimes play their reindeer games is all.*

Rolling her eyes and frowning at the same time, Brynna shoved the thoughts away. No. She didn't have holiday nerves, and she never played games. She was simply ready to once again flee her stifling hometown. Being an invalid sucked, and she'd struggled being back here where everyone had expectations of her. She was ready to leave, and that was that.

Even though, she had to grudgingly admit, Deep Hollow was pretty cute right now. Everything was decorated for Christmas and had been since the day after Thanksgiving. Everyone she saw was cheerful and laughing, beautifully decorated trees were on display in living room windows every night, and carols tinkled from speakers in every store in town. Secretly, so very secretly, she thought it all looked charming. Welcoming. Filled with a bunch of happy *fa la la la la* and abundant joy that actually did lift her spirits. Somewhat.

But all that didn't matter now. She tipped up her chin in determination. She, Brynna Elyse Darby, had a nice life outside of this backwoods little town, and she was going back to it as soon as she could. Her best life was lived far away from this place and its unsettling memories.

This place is home, the whisper inside her came again. *Home.*

She stopped dancing, a small frown drawing down her mouth. That was what she really didn't like to think about. The part of her she wanted to leave behind, trapped back here in Deep Hollow forever. The part with demanding requirements she'd fled years ago. The part of her that had left behind a hometown that thought she should live up to a tradition she wanted nothing to do with.

The part of her that also had left behind a piece of her heart, no matter how darned much she tried to deny it.

A flash of something that felt like pain whipped through her. Sexy blue eyes and amazing lips that could kiss her senseless slipped through her thoughts, making everything inside her squeeze together and suck away her breath.

No. She was done. The other night had proven beyond a shadow of a doubt that she'd made the right decision when she'd left this place years before. She was leaving again, and no one could stop her.

Least of all the sexiest, most irritating, possessive, and downright heart-tugging bear shifter she knew. The panty-melting kiss she'd shared with him the other night had once again rocked her world, but no. She couldn't, she *wouldn't,* go back to this life. She sure as hell wouldn't go back to a— a—a dominating, domineering, jealous jackass of a guy who wanted nothing more than to keep her here and never let her leave again.

Hmph.

She didn't care that he still was the one and only guy in the world who could kiss her with an intensity that made her deeply hidden inner self kick up her heels and do a dance of joy. Brynna Darby wouldn't let anyone tell her how to live her life anymore, and that was that.

Whipping a stiff smile back onto her face, she walked around the pathway railing to drop into some light post-run stretches. "You're awesome, Thor, thanks. You're the best physical therapist in the world, and the best guy I ever could've wanted for Alina. I'll tell her she can keep you," she added with a decisive nod of her head as she stretched her quads.

Thor laughed. "Gee, thanks. Though I'm pretty sure she's already decided to keep me." That dopey smile he wore every time he mentioned Brynna's sister spread over his face as he flashed the engagement band on his left hand.

Brynna's glance flicked to the bright glint of the brushed titanium band that indicated Thor's taken status. Swallowing the sharp lurch of a sigh, she beamed a quick smile before hiding her face between her arms as she grasped the railing and leaned into her stretch. She was utterly thrilled for her sweet sister. But shameful as it was, Brynna couldn't help the tinge of jealousy that her sister had found the perfect man while Brynna was still single.

Stupid, she muttered to herself. She was about to go back to the most amazing, exciting life ever. She didn't need a permanent guy in the whirlwind hustle and bustle of global travel guiding. And it sure wasn't like she pined for a normal existence of being married—*mated,* the internal voice insisted, which made her frown again—complete with white picket fence, a sweet and slightly goofy dog, and a little bun in the oven.

No, Brynna wasn't like her sister, Alina, who was perfectly content to settle down with Thor into just such a normal, simple life here in Deep Hollow. Their lives were complete with stable jobs and a nice little house that did indeed have a white picket fence and a very sweet, goofy golden retriever in residence who didn't mind being owned by two shifters, even if Thor was a hulking bear shifter. And very much unlike Brynna, Alina enjoyed her yearly shifter duties and didn't mind doing them forever.

But not Brynna. Nope. None of that was for her. She'd always had much bigger dreams. The sooner she could get out of Deep Hollow and return to living on her own terms, the better off she'd be.

Then why, she reluctantly mused as she kept stretching, did seeing an engagement ring make her feel wistful? Worse, why did it make her think of that certain pair of brilliant blue eyes, wildly talented lips, muscles that went on for days, and a quick, funny, interesting mind that turned her on like that of no other guy she'd ever met? A guy she thought she'd never see again—until she ran into him just the other night.

She'd felt herself once more falling so hard for Wyatt Webber she was afraid she might never find her way back up. Even if he was the most domineering, possessive, intense guy she'd ever known.

Yes, the voice inside her whispered, very firmly. *Him. Wyatt. He's mine.*

No, she commanded herself back just as firmly, pushing away a nip of pain somewhere in the vicinity of her chest. *Damn you, Wyatt. Damn you for coming back here too.*

Abruptly straightening up, she turned toward the path. "Do you mind if we head back to the cars now? If you're going to clear me, I need to start packing. Today." Without looking at Thor, Brynna slipped around the railing and began to walk with a brisk stride to the small side path that led away from the creek walkway and back to where they'd parked.

"Uh, right now?" he called from behind her, jogging the few steps to catch up. She could hear the confusion in his voice. "But it's Christmas in just a few days. I thought you planned to stick around for that."

A frown creased her face again. "Nope. You know how much I can't stand this time of year."

Well, that's kind of a lie, the voice murmured at her. *You like it. Admit it.*

Not *the* voice, but *her* voice. The part of her she wanted to deny existed. She grunted low in her throat, not even meaning to do so. A peeved little deer grunt.

That was her shifter side. A reindeer shifter. Dumbest shifter type in the world.

An aggravated snort rattled inside, accompanied by what felt like a sharp kick to her thoughts by little deer legs.

It was definitely time to escape this town. Too bad she couldn't really leave behind her shifter side. It might be cute, but she didn't need it out in the world.

Feeling another snort start to bloom inside her, one that threatened to roll out of her mouth, she quickly said out loud to Thor, "You guys can all enjoy Christmas without me being here. Besides, it's not like I've been here for the holidays once ever since I left. Everyone else can handle it without me." She managed to keep her tone light.

Chancing a glance at her future brother-in-law, she saw concern etched over his expression. For some ridiculous reason, that made her even more annoyed. "Christmas isn't my job, Thor!"

Brynna winced. That had come out harsher than she'd intended. "Sorry. I just mean—Deep Hollow isn't my home anymore," she said softly. "Everyone here has to accept that. I'm grateful I could come here to heal, and it was good to spend time with family and old friends, but it was temporary. Now I'm ready to leave. And you yourself said I'm all healed up now, so I can leave."

Silence. Smart man, he didn't press on that touchy subject any longer.

Finally, he just shrugged. "Okay. But you will be back in the spring for the wedding, right?" Slight anxiety tinged his voice. Big bear shifter that he was, her sister had him utterly wrapped around her tiny, cute finger. "Alina will kill me if I said you were ready to go and it meant you were gonna bail on being the maid of honor. This wedding day thing is so important to her that she's kinda turning into a basket case over the details."

Brynna stifled a chuckle at Thor's worried expression. He might be a big, brawny bear shifter, but his tiny mate definitely ruled their little roost. Although shifters usually had a mating ceremony when they cemented their bond, there were so many mixed pairings in this mixed town that most mating ceremonies were now heavily styled after a traditional human wedding. Alina and Thor's wedding was planned for late spring in a huge, blow-out celebration to which practically the entire town had been invited. Alina had definitely gone off the deep end when it came to planning it.

Brynna nodded vigorously. "I'll definitely be

back for that. She'd kill us both if I didn't. I just need to get out of here for now. There's too much —distraction," she settled on after a moment of searching for the right word. *Distraction* was as close as she could come to putting a label on everything that had been spinning uncontrollably inside her since a few nights ago. Distraction with blue eyes and a deep, rumbling voice that could bring her to her little reindeer knees.

Sexy jerk of a bear.

"Sounds good," Thor said, back to his usual easygoing manner. His laid-back, accepting nature was part of the reason Alina liked him, Brynna knew. Simple, uncomplicated, and nice. Just like Alina.

She sighed to herself. She'd never had it so easy. Labeled headstrong and even rebellious since she was little—though she preferred to think of it as being determined and self-assured—Brynna had pushed aside her shifter heritage from the word *go,* making her life crazy complicated in too many ways. After all, she hadn't exactly been asked to be born a reindeer shifter. Being back here now for as long as she had made all those uncomfortable memories crowd into her mind every day, made the little reindeer voice in her head more insistent, and made the differences between herself and every shifter in this town who was completely at peace with themselves that much more pronounced.

Being back here was too freaking hard to deal with, and she was done.

She didn't care that it was Christmas soon, that her family had been excited at the thought of her finally being back here for it. She needed to leave *now*. Especially since those molten eyes she couldn't get out of her head had haunted her every moment since the other night. The eyes that set her on fire and made her want to throw herself into Wyatt's arms like a loony, moony girl instead of the sophisticated world traveler she was now.

Darn that bear shifter and his darned panty-melting ways.

"So," Thor said, pulling up alongside Brynna, shaking her out of her thoughts. "You'll at least stay for our pre-holiday dinner tonight, won't you?" Alina had been planning the casual get-together for weeks. "We could also call it a going-away dinner for you. A temporary going away, that is," he added quickly, laughing as he slung a broth-erly arm around Brynna's shoulders. "We really need to emphasize that to my beloved bride-to-be or else she'll—"

Sudden movement ahead halted them both into wariness. Around a curve in the little side path, a guy almost ran right into them.

Brynna's breath caught in her throat.

His enormous stride somehow took up all the space in the path. Tall, broad, drop-dead gorgeous, with the most intense blue eyes and the faint shadow of a beard Brynna had just recently felt scrape across her face, raising a thousand delicious tingles and the desire to feel it scrape somewhere else on her body too. He wore a ridiculous red t-shirt with the words HOLIDAY MODE: ON written in bright green letters across his very broad chest. The second he laid eyes on Brynna, he stopped dead.

Her heart fluttered in her chest. Stupid little heart. "Wyatt," she breathed, as startled to see him here as he was to see her.

Wyatt, her reindeer echoed, just as taken with him. *Mine.*

What? No, he wasn't *mine.* He was just a part of her ancient history. In fact, he was just a jerk of a guy based on his macho man actions the other night. All brawn and no manners. In fact—

Oh, no. Brynna's insides lurched as Wyatt's eyes narrowed to nearly glowing slits as he stared at Thor. His bear was roused, lurking just beneath the surface. Barely controlled bear. No manners, for sure. Wyatt wasn't just startled to see her here. He was startled to see her here *with another guy*. A guy he didn't know. A guy whose arm was around her shoulders.

Ohhh, shit.

Wyatt's entire face turned to granite. Thor sensed the danger, his companionable arm slipping off of Brynna's shoulders as he tensed. In a split second, Brynna knew exactly what was going to happen. She knew Wyatt far too well, even if it had been almost five years since she'd last spent real time with him.

After all, she'd seen this aggressive, possessive side of him again just a few nights ago.

"Wyatt, don't—" was all she managed to get out before all hell broke loose.

Wyatt lunged forward, mouth opened in a snarl, his hands reaching right for Thor's throat to squeeze the life out of him.

2

W yatt Webber's casual morning trail run was shot all to hell in a split second. He saw red. Not the cheerful red of this holiday season. Nope. This was a roaring, angry blood red.

That was *his* Brynna. His woman. With another man's arm around her shoulders. Brynna was *his,* no one else's. He'd throttle the hell out of anyone who thought otherwise.

His bear rumbled and roared inside him, just as blindly enraged. Wanting blood. Didn't matter that Wyatt had only recently kissed Brynna again for the first time in years. Didn't matter that she itched to leave Deep Hollow in her dust as soon as her doctor or whatever decided her leg was healed.

Didn't matter that attacking someone else in public was a bad idea. Especially for someone like him, a brand new deputy sworn to uphold the public safety.

Fuck all that. The guy with Brynna was one dead male just for daring to breathe in her space, let alone touch her like he was allowed to do so.

Wyatt was the only one who could ever touch her again. Brynna was his—his—

Shit. She was his *what*, exactly?

Mate! he could feel his bear roaring inside.

Not anymore, Wyatt snarled back at himself. Yet his mind eagerly circled the possibility of that word, *mate,* even as his attention was snagged by the shrieking reality of the moment. Literally shrieking.

Apparently, Brynna was his yelling, angry *something* right now.

"Wyatt, stop! What the hell are you doing?" She lunged forward to grab his hands, which were satisfactorily almost closed around the other asshole's throat. "Don't!"

Wyatt felt bright rage grip him harder in his desire to simply protect what was his.

His? What the fuck.

The realization that he was thinking about her in such a possessive way finally managed to douse the flames of his anger. Cursing silently, he forced himself to hold his blazing fury in check. Using every ounce of strength he possessed, he made himself listen to her outrage and stand down.

Hoo, boy. She let loose on him. "You haven't changed one bit! Who the hell made you the head cave bear around here anyway?" Brynna stood with her arms down at her sides, fists clenched, her beautiful little breasts heaving as she yelled. Scrappy and strong, even though she was maybe a hundred pounds soaking wet and barely came up to his chest. Damn cute little reindeer shifter. He'd been in love with her since about the second grade. Small package, but one hell of a big presence.

Even when furious, wow, was she ever gorgeous.

Wyatt couldn't help staring at her as his possessive rage slightly eased with each pound of his fucking dumb heart. Brynna's long brown hair was caught back in a braid, with small strands clinging to her damp forehead. Eyes the color of caramel mocha were stunning even though they snapped with her shocked anger. And that body. The curves he'd been able to touch and stroke for far too short a time the other night taunted him now, displayed under her clinging running pants and a long-sleeved shirt he was almost jealous of for the way it hugged her. She wore nothing else despite the winter chill. Being a shifter, her genetics allowed her to stay warm enough in the late December air, especially since she'd clearly just been exercising. With another man. Another bear shifter, even.

Wyatt's bear roared inside him. The red haze threatened to take over once more. Fuuuck, this woman made him crazy. He literally bit his own tongue to shake himself out of it, forcing his hands to relax away from the other guy's neck. His bear growled inside him, but backed off. For now.

The man he'd been about to strangle huffed out a grunt of anger, holding his ground as he stared back at Wyatt. "What the fuck is your problem," he snarled, his bear rumbling beneath his voice. He was a big guy who clearly had a big bear inside him as well. "I'm gonna pound your dumb ass into the ground, you insane jerk."

Wyatt opened his mouth again to blast out a retort, but Brynna cut him off. "Both of you, stop being such guys," she snapped, the usually creamy-smooth voice that about brought Wyatt to his knees each time he heard it sounding more sandpaper rough at the moment. "What the hell is this, Wyatt? You're acting like a psycho! Thor could call the sheriff and have you charged with assault if you touch him." Her pretty eyes narrowed at him. "Of course, since you're the new deputy here, your po-po buddies probably would make sure the charges wouldn't stick."

Po-po? Despite the situation, Wyatt snorted in some amusement.

Brynna's eyes narrowed even more. Oh, beautiful woman. Pretty little deer shifter. Fuck him, he was halfway to getting a boner just looking at her angry fire right now. What the hell was wrong with him, anyway?

Mate! his bear roared again. *My mate.*

Wyatt tightened his jaw in frustration at that impossibility. No, she wasn't. Not anymore.

Not ever again.

The man she was with interjected. "There won't be any charges, though it's tempting. Idiot," he snapped, glaring at Wyatt. His bear flared bright in his eyes. "I'm not competition. I'm engaged to Brynna's sister. Whom I love dearly and have eyes only for."

He turned his frown on Brynna. "So this block-head is Wyatt, huh? And he's the new deputy here?" Shaking his head, he glared back at Wyatt again. "You need to get a handle on that temper of yours. That's just asking for trouble in these parts."

Wyatt clenched his jaw. "These parts happen to be my hometown. I don't recognize you, which means you didn't grow up here. Everyone here knows me, and that makes me a-okay in 'these parts.' Let me tell you," he added with gravel underscoring his tone, "there won't be any trouble as long as you stay away from her. Do you understand me?" He could hear the edge of his still pissed-off bear in his voice. He didn't care what the guy said, or who he was engaged to. He still was standing way too fucking close to Brynna.

The man opened his mouth again, but this time Brynna jerked her head *no*. "Don't bother, Thor. He's playing over-possessive cave bear again. Something that hasn't changed in the last five years, apparently."

She looked at Wyatt with her chin tipped up a bit, an unconsciously defiant stance that suddenly made him want to smile at how fierce she was. Which was very fierce. And strong. And so fucking sexy he could hardly stand it.

21

He wanted to kiss all the fierce anger and doubt out of her. Kiss her like he had the other night, for the first time in too many years. Just remembering their soul-shaking embrace turned him on to a ridiculous degree right now. He wanted to grab her and pull her close to him while he aimed his lengthening canines for the sweet flesh of her shoulder.

So he could bite her and mark her as his, once and for all.

So he could make her his claimed mate.

Wait, what? *No.*

Wyatt ground his jaw at the bizarre, completely unexpected desire to claim Brynna that had been dogging him ever since he'd reconnected with her. So unexpectedly running into her the other night had been an enormous shock. He'd been so sure she would never return to little Deep Hollow, so sure she was still living the jet-setter life as she led fancy tour groups to the world's famous sites. But when he'd been out on his training run along the riverwalk the other evening, he almost literally ran right into her jogging the opposite direction on the same path.

He'd breathed an unbelieving, "Brynna?" when he saw her. It made her stop short and cock her head at him as she stared back at him. Just as he started to be afraid she was angry to see him, that he was the last person she'd wanted to run into, a huge smile had filled her face, making it shine like all the light of the sun resided within her. "Wyatt," she had breathed back, the sound of his name on her tongue practically setting off fireworks right then and there.

Just like that, he'd been a goner. Hook, line, and sinker. He wanted nothing more than to see that smile again every day of his life, preferably because he was the one to put it on her face.

They'd gone to dinner that same night. She'd told him about the accident she'd been in a few months ago while halfway around the world for work. The sheer grit and determination of her healing journey had impressed him as always. Being a shifter, she had swift healing capabilities. But it had been a really bad fracture, and she hadn't been able to shift into her deer soon enough after it happened to help speed up the process, so it had been a tough recovery. She was fierce and focused, however, and she was indeed recovering. His Brynna was as strong as she was sexy.

They'd gone for a stroll after dinner, and he'd

kissed her, under the half-moonlight along this very riverwalk.

The same riverwalk where they now stood again, both glaring at one another, the air between them zinging with something wild and electrifying, crackling with a tension that made his bear half crazy.

She clearly saw his bear rumbling inside him just below the surface, because her chin tipped up a bit more. A tiny but audible little snort huffed out of her, one filled with judgment about his attitude.

Fine. She thought he was an over-possessive cave bear? No problem. That was something he'd always been good at. Especially around Brynna Darby. Fighting his bear on this was proving impossible.

He had to spend more time with her. No matter what.

"All right, Bryn." She bristled at the familiar way he said it, but he didn't miss the catch in her breath or the sudden, undeniable scent of her arousal. Oh, yeah. No matter what had happened in the past, they were both goners, at least as far as physical attraction to one another went. As for the rest of what was between them—well, that was still to be revealed.

He firmly held her gaze. "Since we've made sure your little tagalong here"—the other bear growled under his breath but kept still—"isn't a problem, you will agree to have dinner with me again. Tonight." His tone said he expected nothing but a *yes* answer.

There, fierce little reindeer. Let's see how you handle that, he thought with a satisfaction that was both grim and somewhat amused. He'd always liked pushing her buttons. Her reaction would be worth it.

Her eyes widened as her mouth dropped open. Then pure fire stormed back into her expression. Her chest heaved with an outraged gasp, and she clenched adorable little fists at her sides.

Before she could answer, Wyatt got jostled from behind. Whipping around to level a glare at the other shifter who'd just smacked into him, he growled in irritation. His cousin and running buddy ignored him and looked curiously past Wyatt, then made a noise of understanding.

"Hey, Brynna." Slade Walker nodded at her as he stepped up beside Wyatt. "This dickhead giving you any trouble?"

Wyatt snapped his head back around just in time to see Brynna's full lips twitch. She snorted, then shook her head. "Hi, Slade. No, he's just making trouble for himself. Same as always." She leveled a pointed glare at Wyatt. "It seems he never grew out of it."

Slade nodded seriously. "Yeah. Fatal disease for him, troublemaking." He jabbed Wyatt in the side and gave him a stern look. "You hear that, World Wide Web? You're gonna troublemake yourself into an early grave."

Brynna's anger seemed to pause. "You guys still call him that?" A sudden, reminiscent smile turned up her lips.

Wyatt caught his breath. *Yes.* Finally, Brynna was smiling, full and open, right at him. He felt his possessive rage fully slip away in the face of the stunning beauty that was Brynna Darby. She was the cutest, sexiest little reindeer shifter he'd ever met. Not like he'd met that many, since reindeer shifters were rare. But she was definitely the cutest and sexiest one of them all.

His sudden high spirits couldn't be dampened even when the guy still too close to Brynna snorted, "World Wide Web? Why do you call him that?"

Brynna's face bloomed like a gorgeous flower as she still smiled. It was genuine. She wasn't nearly as pissed anymore. "Childhood nickname. Because his name is Wyatt Walker Webber. We turned it into World Wide Web when we were all kids." Her smile got even more real. "Wyatt Walker Webber," she said again softly, studying him with that smile still lifting her pretty lips.

Wyatt felt a shiver of delight tiptoe up and down his spine at the sound of his full name rolled in her mouth, kissed by her lips. Shiiit. He was so screwed.

Her smile light up the cold day. "I guess it stuck. I almost forgot about it."

The stark tension had disappeared. Wyatt took a deep breath, exhaling it slowly. Yeah, picking a fight practically in the middle of town wasn't a good idea. As an esteemed member of Deep Hollow's po-po department, he definitely couldn't go around terrorizing the very citizens he was supposed to protect. He needed to chill the hell out. Now that Brynna was smiling at him, no longer yelling at him, Wyatt could let himself relax.

"Look, I'm sorry I was a dick." Relaxed or not, that was hard to say. He ignored Slade's huffed snort. Slade always called him *dick* anyway, like it was his name or something. He forced himself to stick out his hand to the guy next to Brynna, Thor or whatever. "I'm Deputy Webber. But just call me Wyatt. You are?"

With a final glance at Brynna, the guy shrugged and stuck out his own hand to meet Wyatt's in a strong but friendly grip. "I'm Thor Calhoun. Almost Brynna's brother-in-law. So your middle name's Walker, huh?"

Wyatt nodded.

"You happen to be related to the Walker clan?" Thor's voice stayed casual, though his eyes sized Wyatt up with some new respect. Then he glanced at Slade, who was a Walker himself. The Walkers were held in high regard here in Deep Hollow.

Wyatt nodded again. "Yup. Slade is my cousin. One of several. My dad's sister is Elodie Walker. I grew up here. Left for a job somewhere else years ago." He didn't look at Brynna when he said that. "I just came back here a few weeks ago when I landed the open deputy position. I'm home to stay now," he couldn't help adding. He'd said that to Brynna the other night at dinner, but he felt the strong need to remind her for whatever reason. His bear muttered inside him.

Thor grunted, but he sounded a lot calmer

now. "Elodie Walker's your aunt, huh? And Slade here is your cousin. Along with that whole passel of Walkers."

Both Wyatt and Slade nodded. There were a bunch of Walkers who called Deep Hollow their home. Brothers, cousins, and other extended relatives who all made up a big clan here.

Completely simmered down now, Thor nodded. "Okay then. I guess you might not be a total asshole if you're a Walker. I've only lived her a couple years myself, but I know the Walkers. They're good folks."

Elodie and her mate Oberon Walker were well-known and highly respected in Deep Hollow. This was their clan's home, their territory as grizzly bear shifters. Wyatt didn't usually play that relationship card, but it was smoothing over the moment. Besides, Brynna was right. He had to remember he was a sheriff's deputy here now. He had an image to uphold, and a clan relationship that he needed to keep clean and upstanding, temper or no.

Thor grinned suddenly. He actually seemed like a pretty friendly guy. "Welcome home, then. It's a good time of year to be here," he added in an even more cheerful tone. "Christmas in this town is the best."

An abrupt silence thunked over them, awkward and uncomfortable. Fuuuck. Wyatt didn't look at Brynna. He could sense her determinedly not looking at him, either. Even Slade, who of course knew their personal backstory, seemed suddenly uncomfortable, while Thor looked confused at the stiff silence.

Great.

Wyatt loved Christmas in Deep Hollow, and always had ever since he was a cub. He loved the sparkle and jingle of the holiday. The way Main Street was lit from end to end with colorful lights draped over the street signs, the lamp posts, the sidewalk benches and all the business windows. It was dumb, but he'd also always loved caroling, and drinking hot cider in front of a crackling fire, and the smell of fresh pine needles as everyone hung wreaths on doorways. Christmas had always been his favorite time of the year, and he fell for its charms like a total sucker every December.

But the last time he'd seen Brynna, before the other night, had been on Christmas Eve five years ago. That one night had ruined his Christmases for a long time afterward. The memory of that brutally painful time smashed over him like an unrelenting wave of pure misery.

It had been a week before he was set to leave for Montana to go to his first real job, and he'd planned for that Christmas Eve to be the most spectacular one he or Brynna had ever had. He knew she'd never liked that time of year, and he understood why, but he'd been so damned pleased with his idea, so certain she'd love it, that he couldn't help himself. He'd dressed up as Santa, complete with the classic red hat on his head and a white wig and beard set he'd picked up at one of the local shops.

His big plan was to give her a Christmas gift she'd always remember: a stunning engagement ring. That night, under the decorated tree twinkling in his little apartment in downtown Deep Hollow, he would ask Brynna to come with him to Montana, ring on her finger, and make him the happiest bear on the planet.

Well, that was a big, fat nope.

Cute little Brynna Darby, fuckin' love of his life and definitely his mate, had broken up with him on Christmas Eve instead.

"I'm sorry, Wyatt," she'd said, her eyes shining with tears even as she stood firm. "I just can't go with you." She said she needed more from life than being a reindeer shifter, living in little towns that had ridiculous expectations of her every holiday season. She wasn't about to move from tiny Deep Hollow, Colorado, to equally tiny Snowhaven, Montana, just to follow Wyatt.

Not even if she loved him with all her heart, which he knew for a damn fact she did. Brynna Darby was his mate, and they both knew it.

But a place called Snowhaven probably had even more crazy Christmas celebrations than Deep Hollow anyway, and who wanted that? Not Brynna Darby, reluctant reindeer shifter. A shifter who'd never left Deep Hollow and was itching to see what the rest of the world might offer. She needed more than Wyatt could offer her, she'd said, even though tears had started to stream down her face.

Then she'd up and really destroyed him.

After saying no to his romantic holiday proposal, she had even more news for him. Since he'd already told her he was leaving Deep Hollow and she had nothing else to keep her there anymore, she'd secretly applied for and then accepted a job based in Miami as an international tour guide for an upscale company.

Fuckin' *Florida.* Far from winter, other reindeer, and holiday traditions like the ones in Deep Hollow.

Far from Wyatt.

Yeah, that had stung. Real bad. Worst Christmas ever, and it had soured him on the season for a while.

So he'd left for Snowhaven all by his lonesome, made himself lose touch with her, and didn't keep up on news about her from her family and friends still in Deep Hollow. He just sucked it up like the big bear shifter he was and forced himself to focus on his new life. He'd worked damn hard over the past several years to forget Brynna, and he'd practically succeeded, even though his bear had never been quite the same.

But then the other night happened. Oh, yeah. The other night.

Sexy, sexy little Brynna that night. Running into her all unexpectedly had brought back every single memory he had of all the time they'd ever spent together, which was basically their entire lives. Then the kiss. Hell, yeah. His whole body tingled right now just remembering it. It was just a kiss, but it had lit something between them again. And that was saying a lot, considering how many times he'd been privileged enough to kiss Brynna in the past. But hell. He couldn't focus on that too much right now, or he'd get a freaking boner for sure. Just like damned teenager again.

Quickly, before the moment could get any more stupid awkward, Wyatt went in the other direction. Caveman style, all the way. He looked square at Brynna and said, "So what do you say, Bryn? Dinner? Tonight." He shoved as much bold assurance into his voice as he could. He was still pushing her buttons a bit, yeah. But he also meant it. He'd pissed her off the other night, and again now. He honestly wanted a chance to make it good between them again. The holiday season was giving him confidence.

Brynna stayed quiet for a moment, then dragged her eyes to his. Her irritation was gone, and something else flared in her expression.

After she paused too long, Thor nudged her. "Come on, Bryn, tell him what's up." The guy flashed a quick glance at Wyatt before he looked away. An almost sympathetic glance.

Shit.

Taking a breath, the sexiest little reindeer shifter in the world opened her mouth and once again rocked Wyatt's world. Badly. "I'm sorry,

Wyatt, I can't have dinner with you. I'm all healed up as of today. So I'm ready to go back to where I live now. In Florida," she added, as if he might have forgotten. "I'm packing my stuff tonight and hitting the road soon. I'm leaving Deep Hollow, Wyatt," she finished in what was almost a whisper.

Another fucking awkward silence landed like a dirty bomb. Wyatt could sense both Thor and Slade itching to just turn and bolt away.

He looked right at Brynna. "It's almost Christmas, Bryn." His voice was soft, but there was a sharp edge under it that he couldn't quite control.

She swallowed hard, nodding. "Yes." A very faint wobble stuttered through her voice. But her gaze stayed firm.

The world narrowed in on Wyatt. Brynna kept her gaze locked on his. Something flickered in her pretty eyes that he couldn't quite read, but she didn't say anything more. She didn't need to.

Right. The other night with her, brief as it had been, had given him hope again. Stupid, idiotic hope. Because Wyatt's burning, nearly unstoppable desire to protect this woman, and his bear's fierce, nearly overwhelming urge to claim her, told him something he couldn't deny.

35

Sexy, fiery, amazing Brynna was still his mate. Always had been, and always would be.

But even so, even though he knew it and she knew it and everyone in town probably knew it, that still didn't seem to matter to her. She was still leaving both Deep Hollow and him. Again.

Fuck his life, and fuck Christmas.

3

B rynna tossed things into her suitcase like she had a herd of merry reindeer chasing her down trying to throw jingle bells on her tail. Her parents were both out of the house, which made this activity much easier. She wouldn't have to deal with their disappointment at her leaving before Christmas, at least not until later.

What did make this activity much harder was the picture of Wyatt's face she had in her mind that wouldn't leave her alone. His expression when she told him she was leaving again—oh, that hurt. She'd socked him in the gut with it, and the pain she could sense in him hurt her too.

"Not fair," she whispered to herself as she carelessly flung a sweater into her wildly disorganized suitcase. She was never this disorganized. As an experienced traveler, she'd long ago learned to pack little, and to pack smart. But that didn't matter right now. She just needed to get all of her things gathered up and ready to go, so she could zoom out of here.

So she could leave Deep Hollow, her shifter background, and Wyatt behind for good.

Why? It came up inside her more like a feeling than a question. Her reindeer, filled with just as much angst and confusion and sorrow as Brynna felt.

She stopped her packing and moved over to the window to look out into the back yard. Snow filled it, along with enough holiday decorations to rival what was in the front yard. She couldn't help a tiny smile. Her parents were just as Christmas-crazy as Wyatt and always had been.

Why did she want to leave? Good question, but there was an equally good answer.

"Because there's too much pressure here," she answered herself as well as her despairing reindeer. "Because everyone always expects me to be someone, and something, I never asked to be." Her voice had dropped into a whisper. She leaned against the wall, still staring out into the yard.

"He just expected I'd move to Montana with him." She almost shouted now. "Montana! The middle of nowhere. Another shifter town." Her voice softened as she continued her one-sided conversation with herself and her now very silent reindeer. "He assumed I'd go with him, but he never asked me what I wanted to do. And," her chest suddenly heaved as the old, buried pain crawled up, "that really hurt."

Brynna stood quietly for several long moments, slowly breathing in and out, unable to keep the sadness from washing over her. She'd pushed it away for a long time, but seeing Wyatt not once but twice in less than a week apparently had broken all the protective barriers she'd erected against it.

Damned sexy bear shifter, showing up back in town and making her look at her own shit. It sucked. She'd been running from it for a long time, and that had been easy to do.

Right now, this was anything but easy. Yet for some reason, it felt absolutely crucial to go through it. She forced herself to feel all the ancient hurt. To let it open up all the things she'd kept hidden inside for years. To let them out in the open so the light could shine on everything she'd shoved away.

Finally, so deep inside herself, so quietly, she admitted the biggest thing. The thing so big she couldn't say it out loud, not even to herself.

I wanted to leave because he didn't stop me from moving across the country back then. He just let me go, and he never came to get me back.

Oh, that was big. Big, scary, and true. But ah, dang. There was more.

I wanted to leave because he was my mate, and he broke my heart by not proving that. By not claiming me, by just letting me leave instead. Like it didn't really matter to him.

That was even worse. Even more true.

Now came the hardest part. The part she was responsible for all on her own. Brynna let out a shaky breath as she forced herself to face her own failure.

But I didn't go after him either so he would know for sure I was his. Because I was too afraid to admit how much I needed him.

Oh, wow. Gut punch, that one was.

Blinking her eyes fast to hold back the prickling that surged forth, she stayed by the window for several more moments, arms clutched tight around herself. When she could finally see again without an ocean of tears making everything blurry, she slowly unwrapped her arms and turned back to her packing.

She'd known when she came back home to recuperate from her injury that Wyatt wasn't here. But running into him the other evening, when they'd ended up having dinner together, had been one giant shocker. She'd texted Alina from dinner, asking why she hadn't told Brynna he was back in town. But she couldn't blame her sister. Alina hadn't known that he'd just moved back.

Being with Wyatt again, kissing him again, feeling his hard, strong body pressed closely against hers, made it all come flooding back.

The heartbreak when they'd gone their separate ways five years ago.

The pain that she'd never been able to make a real connection with another guy since Wyatt.

Not just because she was independent and knew she didn't need a man to complete her or whatever. No, it was because, as her heart and her reindeer side had always tried to tell her, Wyatt was her other half. Her soul.

Her mate.

The knowledge of that truth had seemed to

threaten everything she wanted for herself. Wyatt wanted to stay in a cute little mountain town like Deep Hollow forever, and Brynna wanted more. So much more. And she didn't want to be a reindeer shifter, darn it. Or rather, she didn't want to deal anymore with the annual holiday demands on reindeer shifters. Been there, done that, got the jingle bells to prove it. Ugh. No thanks. Not her jam at all. Her jam was taking people on tours all over the wide, exciting world instead.

But like the scared girl she'd been, she'd instead made the excuse it was all Wyatt's fault. That he was an arrogant, pushy jerk by getting all snarly at that other random guy. She'd run away from Wyatt yet again the other night like all the demons in hell were after her, instead of only his startled, upset "Brynna!" chasing her down the street under the pale fingers of the half moonlight.

Just like she'd run from him again today, telling him she was leaving. Marching off without a backward glance.

Because if she'd looked back, she would have thrown away all her dreams and leapt into his big, strong arms, asking him to hold her forever and never let her go again.

Brynna squeezed her eyes shut. Her entire body

felt rattled. Taking several deep breaths in and exhaling long and slow, she managed to calm herself. When she opened her eyes again, her gaze landed on the calendar on the wall above the desk. Squaring her shoulders, she walked over to it. Paris gleamed brightly from the December image, sparkling and shiny and enticing. Brynna loved Paris. It was a fun, vibrant city.

Fun to fly over, her incessant little inner voice murmured.

Well. Yes, she'd shifted into her reindeer very late one night when she'd been there and flown over the beautiful city, admiring its stunning array of lights. It had been very fun to fly over it.

Not that she would ever tell anyone she'd done so. As a rare reindeer shifter, she'd been born with the ability to fly as well as pull a sleigh through the sky. Just because she didn't want to *have* to do that once a year didn't mean she didn't like to fly around at night every now and again.

Just because she didn't want to embrace the shifter part of her life didn't mean she totally denied it.

A little snort deep inside dripped with cynicism.

Crinkling her brow, Brynna heaved a big sigh

as she forced herself to woman the hell up and admit yet more truths to herself.

"I don't hate being a reindeer shifter," she murmured to the empty room at large. "And..." She hesitated.

Slowly, she reached for the large black marker on her desk. With a precise hand, she crossed off today's date, just like all the days in the many weeks before had been crossed off ever since she'd hobbled back home. She'd been counting them down till she could leave Deep Hollow. The X she squeaked over the calendar now was on the 23rd. Slowly, she reached out to it, her fingers lingering on tomorrow's date. The 24th of December.

Christmas Eve.

Just a holiday. Not the end of the world. Just a holiday that was very important to those she loved. Just a holiday she didn't actually hate. It was just a little—much.

Her reindeer harumphed again, but it sounded more hopeful.

Brynna sighed. Yes, she could wait a little longer. Not just because it was almost Christmas Eve, and her family had gently, hopefully been wanting her to stay for it. But also because the pure, undeniable truth was this: Wyatt was *her* bear.

Wyatt-the-ultra-annoying-and-heartbreaking-bear-shifter-Webber was her man, her bear, her mate. She did know that. She could acknowledge that.

And maybe she owed it to Wyatt to make the memories of this holiday season a good one, instead of dashing it all to dust yet again. Maybe she owed that to both of them.

"Yes," she whispered. "Okay. I'll stay a little longer."

As a hint of smile lifted her lips, tiny hooves seemed to dance through her heart, clattering with joy.

4

The Deep Hollow sheriff's department looked like Christmas had thrown up all over it. Twinkling lights, decals of sleighs and toys and snowmen on office windows, holiday music floating out of every room.

Wyatt's jaw twitched as he strode down the main hallway. Christmas Eve should be one of his favorite days of the year, but all it was doing to him right now was making him want to punch something. Probably himself, if he was truthful. Good thing the department was closing early today, and he wasn't on duty over the holiday. He was off the clock in half an hour. Then he'd make his way to one of the bars in town and drink himself into oblivion. An oblivion that would black out any and all thoughts of Brynna and that she was probably already on a plane, headed back to Florida.

And then there was the gawky young shifter jogging along behind Wyatt. He growled under his breath. He wanted to swat the kid away, like he was a fly. A rookie deputy here, the kid had attached himself like a barnacle to Wyatt right after he'd moved back to town a few weeks earlier. He couldn't even remember the kid's name, but the kid sure knew who he was. Everyone in the department did.

Word of Wyatt's stellar record back at his old department in Montana had preceded him, especially his feat saving that little boy from drowning in the local river late last summer after a huge storm had swelled the water over its banks. He did so-called hero shit like that simply because his job meant he was supposed to serve and protect. Not because he wanted a worshipful young shifter dogging his every step. He couldn't even tell what kind of shifter the guy was, but he was on the small side. Probably some kind of rodent shifter, for crying out loud.

"Did your paperwork come through yet, Wyatt? I bet you'll be starting any day now. Sure hope we can be partners out on patrol beats." The kid was all animation as Wyatt strode down the hallway to his office. "I'm fast, and I pay attention, and I got good commendations during the last evaluation period. I'm ready to step up and learn from the best," he added so seriously that Wyatt almost choked trying to hold in his disbelieving snort. Instead, he grunted something noncommittal and walked faster.

He was not long past the rookie stage himself, having completed his grueling first years back in Snowhaven. He'd gotten restless there, though, and when the time came for him to move up in the ranks, he'd instead decided to come back home when the deputy position opened up here. He'd always loved Deep Hollow, and he still had family here. Being a deputy in a tiny shifter town like Snowhaven was exactly what he loved to do, but he'd realized in the last few years that he missed his own tiny shifter hometown, not to mention his family and old friends. Being back in the Colorado mountains felt damned good. When the job here came available, it had been a clear sign to him that he was meant to come home.

The fact that Brynna wasn't here anymore had made his decision to return all the easier. Until, of course, he realized she was here, and all the old shit between them had come roaring to the surface again. Now his entire being seemed to see-saw with confusion and doubt. But damn it all, he was home, he was settled here, and he wasn't about to leave again. Brynna was the one leaving Deep Hollow again. He'd eventually calm back down to the smooth-running, emotion-ignoring life he'd been leading for the past several years. He could handle this, damn it all.

His bear grumped inside him. Wyatt bit back a growl, walking even faster as the memories of yesterday washed over him again. Slade had peeled off after their run, happily saying something about needing to go see his mate. The quietly thrilled smile on his face as he said it made Wyatt wince. Hell, he was glad his cousin recently had claimed his mate, but he had admit it smarted to see the happy couples that seemed to be everywhere he looked lately. They strolled along the town's little Main Street arm in arm, shopping for gifts and kissing under the mistletoe that had sprouted seemingly overnight above a lot of business doorways in town.

Kinda made a bear grouchier than usual. Especially with Brynna's damned bombshell announce-

J.K. HARPER

ment that she was out of here once again. After she'd said a stiff good-bye, she'd quickly whipped around and marched away down the path. Thor had followed her with another sympathetic glance at Wyatt.

After a long moment, Wyatt and Slade had continued their own run, Slade almost dragging a numb Wyatt along. "Don't make it worse right now," he'd said with the kind of wisdom possessed only by a bear with a mate. "Sorry, man."

"Yeah," Wyatt had grunted in return, his entire body buzzing with the need to run after Brynna and grab her. He'd instead decided being crazy twice in one day wasn't too smart, and forced himself to keep running with Slade. He had some damned pride. He wasn't chasing after a woman who didn't want him. A woman who had kissed him the other night like he was the air to her breath, then up and just decided to leave.

Well. He'd been a possessive grump that night, too. His bear knew Brynna was his mate, and once his bear had his sights set on something, it was hard to rein him in. But Wyatt had spent a lot of time the past few years working on that side of his personality. He'd made strides and was a lot calmer now, more methodical about responding instead of reacting.

Except, apparently, when he once again saw the woman who was the mate his bear refused to let him truly forget.

Gritting his teeth, he'd forced himself to keep running. Slade was a wildland firefighter who needed to stay in good shape, which made him a great running partner. They usually didn't talk much during runs, just pushed each other hard, thereby ensuring they got their training time in. But Slade had decided to be a damned chatterbox that morning. "Looks like Brynna still hates being a reindeer shifter," he'd offered out of nowhere. He and Brynna had also known one another since they were kids, both having been raised in Deep Hollow.

Startled, Wyatt had almost stumbled over a crusty pile of snow kicked into the path. "How do you get that?"

Slade ran around a small pack of moms and kids meandering down the walkway, filled with red cheeks and giggling shrieks and laughter. "Because she's leaving town again right now. You know how much she always hated Christmas. She's bailing back to the land of palm trees and beaches."

"Pretty sure people celebrate Christmas in Miami," Wyatt pointed out, breathing hard as the river path began angling upward as they neared the top of town. "They just decorate palm trees instead of pine trees."

Exhaling as they reached the end of the run, Slade shook his head. "You were too busy getting all googly-eyed over her to pay attention."

"Googly-eyed?" Wyatt demanded, slowing down.

Somberly, Slade nodded. "You couldn't take your eyes off of her, and you went kind of all soft in the face, even when she was yelling at you. I look at Everly that way all the time," he added, his own face definitely going soft as he smiled. His mate sure had brought out the mushy side in Slade.

"Whatever." Wyatt shook his head, ignoring his bear's huffs of agreement. "Googly-eyed, my ass. I just—Brynna and I used to be close, is all. You know we were super tight when we were all kids." *And when she and I were grown ups, too,* he wanted to add, but didn't. Damn if it didn't hurt way too fucking much to think about that.

Slade just snorted. "Face up to the truth, won't you? She's still the one you want, Wyatt. Fucking hell, man." Slade shot him a hard glance. "She's your mate. Always has been."

Wyatt frowned. "We were pretty good friends. That's all. She shared a lot of stuff with me."

"Mm-hmm. Right." Slade's tone had been speculative. "But how much did you share with her?"

That was a gut punch. Because the answer was, *Everything*. Wyatt had shared everything with her.

He had never had any secrets from Brynna. They were always friends, just kids playing in literal sandboxes and then riding bikes in their neighborhood. She'd been his little shadow, following him everywhere, trying everything he did, even if it was kind of scary. Like climbing trees to the very top, or leaping off the swings at their apex and flying through the sky to land on the hard ground. She'd been cool, though, and a total tomboy. Fearless and daring, she could keep up with all the older kids on their bikes, swimming in the river, running around playing mock battle games in the woods.

Their dinner the other night had proved she'd forgotten nothing about them being best friends growing up. And about how deep their serious dating relationship had been when they were old enough to look at one another that way.

And that they were mates.

Then like a damn fool he'd gone and pissed her off, behaving like a maniacal caveman that night by growling and lunging at a guy who looked twice at her while she and Wyatt strolled along the riverwalk. She'd stormed off, snapping over her shoulder if he wasn't ready to be an adult, she didn't need to spend any time with him again.

He'd planned and plotted every second since then to see her again, but running into her on the same riverwalk just a few days later had been a very unexpected, welcome surprise. Until he'd gone all jackass on her yet again.

He shook his head in savage fury. Letting her go was the smartest thing to do. Except—he had to see her again. Something deep inside told him if he didn't, he was blowing the biggest thing that would ever happen to him in his entire life. Such as acknowledging to himself and everyone else the truth that she was his mate. His actual mate, damn it all. He couldn't let her go again. It would kill him, slowly but surely. Even if it was Christmas-time again, and the memories of that last Christmas when she'd smashed his heart were rearing up fast and ugly in his head.

That had been enough heartbreak for one lifetime. Right? Right.

By the time they reached the top of the riverwalk, ignoring his bear's decidedly unhappy grumbles, he turned his thoughts around to practicality. No. He couldn't risk his dumb heart being shattered yet again, and especially not again at his favorite time of year. He was just beginning a new life here in Deep Hollow. He'd bought a frigging house. His family and old friends were happy to have him back. Holiday merriment abounded all around him, and he just didn't have the bandwidth for more fuckin' trauma in the form of a sexy, frustrating little deer shifter who didn't want to stay here.

So when he and Slade finished their run yesterday, Wyatt had decisively stated, "I'm letting go of it all. I've got no time for a woman who's got no time for me."

Slade snorted a doubtful laugh. He shook his head as they went headed into the festively decorated town. "You're like a teeter-totter of confusion. So even though you were about ready to drag her to dinner again, now you're done? For sure?" His skeptical tone messed with Wyatt's newly-arrived decision.

Wyatt growled under his breath. "I'm done. Don't push," he warned.

His cousin just shrugged. "Guess she did a number on you for sure. Sorry," he said again, a glimmer of compassion in his voice. Before Wyatt could growl again, Slade added, "Holidays should be fun, anyway. Yeah, let go of the past and all that. Move on and enjoy yourself. Good plan." His tone still sounded a bit skeptical, but Wyatt ignored it.

The past was the past. He was for damn sure moving on. He'd have a merry Christmas this year or else.

Now, when he reached his office, he shoved aside the events of yesterday and firmly set his mind to paperwork. He did manage a faint smile at the sight of his door, which was decorated with a snowman made from paper and plastic. His niece and nephew, the kids of his oldest sister, had helped. They'd added a long piece of red tinsel around the entire door, with the words ho ho ho! spelled out in green tinsel on it as the final touch. Decorating his door as well as his office in the most over-the-top way of anyone else here had already made the entire sheriff's department christen Wyatt "Santa."

Of course he loved it, though right now it just made him want to "bah, humbug" them all.

He jumped when the rookie kid he'd almost forgotten about uttered a sudden "Sir" behind him, as crisp and clean as any ranking officer could want. Wyatt turned around to see Slade bearing down on them, his expression so bright he about glowed. Slade's wildland fire-fighting team office was attached to the town fire station, which was situated right beside the sheriff's department.

Slade rolled his eyes at the kid, since he was nobody's "sir," but just grunted, "Hey, Deputy Donner."

Right, the kid's name was Donner. Wyatt should remember that.

"Need something?" Wyatt side-eyed Slade's crazy big grin. Huh. Something weird was up.

"We've got a new plan!" Slade's voice rapped out so cheerfully it turned the heads of some administrative staff members chatting down the hall.

Wyatt shook his head, completely lost. "Was there an old plan?"

Slade drew to a stop in front of the door, awarding both Wyatt and rookie Donner a wide grin. "So Alina is friends with Everly, right?" Fox shifter Everly and her family owned a local restaurant and bar called The Tank. Everyone in town knew them.

Wyatt frowned at him. "Uh...okay. So?"

"So," Slade said in a voice that was both patient and pleased at once, "Everly just called Alina to find out what's going on with Brynna."

"Are you fucking kidding me," Wyatt muttered. This was beginning to sound like a game of telephone. Or like any moment back in high school. Small town gossip wasn't something anyone here could escape. But it was usually friendly, plus he could tell Slade was genuinely excited about something. Holding back an irritated growl, he made himself listen.

"Brynna didn't leave town, Wyatt." Slade's grin got even bigger as he said those words.

Battling a sudden surge of hope, Wyatt scrubbed at his neck as he peered at his cousin. The rookie kid stood nearby, eagerly soaking up every word. "No. She said she was hauling ass out of here as soon as she could. She's gone already." Fucking slam to the heart to say that out loud.

Exasperated, Slade shook his head. "No, man. Listen to me. She's still here." He whispered the last few words like they were the key to the universe.

Wyatt's bear sat up to attention. "So? Her family probably talked her into staying for dinner with them tonight. Christmas Eve and all that."

His bear moaned with sadness inside him, though the sharp attention was still there.

The rookie kid's head swung from Slade to Wyatt and back again, listening to personal shit that was none of his business. But Wyatt was too damned intrigued by what Slade was saying to shoo the kid off.

"You're not getting this." Slade shook his head in despair at Wyatt's apparent obtuseness.

"Clearly not." Still trying to squelch the dumb hope springing around inside his chest, Wyatt turned back to his door, opening it and striding into his equally holiday-happy small office. He frowned at the sight of a tiny plastic reindeer prancing on his desktop. The piped station he'd left playing on the crappy little portable radio sitting on a shelf tinnily warbled "Blue Christmas." His frown deepened.

"Wyatt," Slade said, following him in, "Brynna is still here."

Wyatt closed his eyes and ground his jaw. Before he could respond, Slade plowed on.

"She could have left yesterday. Or today. But

she didn't. Are you getting this, finally?" Slade crossed his arms and frowned at Wyatt's apparently idiotic lack of understanding.

Wyatt's bear rumbled inside him. Wyatt ignored it and blindly messed around on his desk, pretending to be looking for something. "So?" he said, hitching up a shoulder in a shrug. Inside, his heart thudded hard against his ribs. Damned fool heart.

"So," rookie Donner blurted out, making both Slade and Wyatt turn their heads to look at him where he stood in the doorway, "she's waiting another day because she wants another chance with you!"

Slade barked out a laugh of approval, unfolding his arms to clap the small kid on his back and nearly knocking him over. Deputy Donner turned cherry red, abruptly shuffling his feet and looking downward. Wyatt just blinked hard for a few seconds.

"Yes!" Slade grinned big again. "That's exactly what Alina told Ever. So Brynna hates the holidays, right?"

Wyatt nodded, his heart still slamming in his chest as his mind suddenly began to spin.

"And she told you she was antsy having been back here so long, right?"

"Yeah."

"And much as she loves her family, they've been able to hang out with her over a month now. Almost two months. So there's no need for big good-byes, no need to drag it out more. Right?"

"Right," Wyatt said, feeling oddly light-headed as his mind began to grasp what Slade was saying.

"So, dick," Slade said cheerfully, "that means she's waiting for only one thing, even if she didn't say it out loud. She's waiting for you," he jabbed a finger into Wyatt's chest, "to get your head out of your ass and tell her you both know that you're hers and she's yours. That you want her to stay here. Or if she won't, that you'll follow her anywhere she goes."

"Wait," Wyatt said in an automatic yet half-hearted protest. "I just got back here. I have a great job. Deep Hollow is my home."

Slade smiled despairingly at him, like he was a little slow. Or a lot slow. "Nah. Deep Hollow is your hometown. It's where you're from. But Brynna is your mate. That means *she's* your true home," he said with a soft smile plastering itself on him, his face going all mushy as he probably thought of his own mate. "Wherever your mate is, *that's* your real home. You have a chance now to make up for five years ago."

Deputy Donner nodded his head like a weeble-wobble, his face as bright with happiness as Wyatt felt.

"Wyatt, you dumb dick." Slade shook his head again, though he looked compassionate. "You never went after her when she left town all those years ago. You think that didn't break her heart too?"

Wyatt felt all the blood surge to his head as Slade's words knocked into him like a major truth bomb. His bear rumbled inside him, suddenly very alert and close to the surface.

Holy shit.

Brynna was his home. She always had been. He'd just thought since she wouldn't come with him when he'd left Deep Hollow those many years ago, it meant they weren't meant to be. But no. He'd bet his entire career, his entire life, that she'd wanted *him* to come with *her*. She'd been too young and scared back then to admit it, not to mention just tired of living here in Deep Hollow, and he'd just been too stubborn, too damned butt hurt, to see it.

Brynna was his mate. And it was about time he man up to that reality and finally do something about it.

Suddenly turning, he raced out of his office and sprinted blindly down the hallway, heedlessly ignoring the confused exclamations that breezed in his desperate wake.

"Where are you going?" Slade called behind him.

"To go get her," Wyatt shouted into the echoing halls. "To get that damned amazing woman, and not let her go again."

Slade whooped, the sound urging Wyatt on to go find the most stubborn little reindeer shifter in the world and this time, give her and him both the best Christmas Eve ever.

Brynna Darby was his mate, and they both knew it. He was never, ever letting her go again. This time, he really would claim her.

Only if, the quiet whisper of doubt rippled in his head, she would let him.

5

Brynna frowned at herself in the mirror. "I'm not seeing it."

Behind her, Alina rolled her eyes, visible in the mirror. "How can you not see it? I swear, you're glowing. You're all glow-y and stuff. Oh, wait!" She gasped dramatically, pausing with her sharp little scissors in one hand and a hank of Brynna's long hair in the other. "You're not pregnant, are you?" She squealed like a high school girl instead of a woman over thirty. "Brynna Darby, my sweet lil sis! Did you and Wyatt do the nasty the other night after all? Oh, you can't leave now! Tell me everything!"

A rousing chorus of "Let It Snow!" rang out from the speakers in Alina's little hair salon, much too cheerfully for the moment. Exasperated, Brynna leveled a death glare at her sister's ridiculously bubbly excitement. "No, I am *not* pregnant. You have babies on the brain."

Alina and Thor planned to have a whole passel of kids, and Alina had already designed the little nursery in their cute house with the white picket fence. Decals of adorable little bears and prancing little reindeer adorned the walls. It was stupid cute. Brynna pretended to sort of hate it, but she really sort of loved it. She was excited to be an aunt. And maybe, one day, she'd design her own nursery.

But not with Wyatt-the-ultra-annoying-and-heartbreaking-bear-shifter-Webber, unless she and he could both un-screw-up everything they'd screwed up so far.

"Spill," Alina commanded breathlessly as she went back to trimming Brynna's hair. She'd insisted that Brynna couldn't leave Deep Hollow without a fresh new cut.

Brynna wasn't really the type of person to always have perfect hair and nails. But that kind of stuff was important to Alina, and Alina was important to Brynna, so she'd made an effort to let her sister keep her hair healthy since she'd been back in Deep Hollow. Besides, it was Christmas Eve today. She was still feeling a little leery of the holiday, but she had to admit it was nice that her family was so thrilled she was staying through the holidays after all, and it was nice to get her hair all dolled up for the day and evening.

All she had to do now was figure out how to explain to Wyatt what she was feeling. What she was wanting. How to tell him she never should have left him all those years ago. Her entire being was still roiling with all of her admissions to herself yesterday, processing it all.

She didn't want to screw things up with him again. She had to figure out how to do it just right, and for all she knew, getting a nice haircut beforehand would make things easier. She nervously giggled to herself as her reindeer pattered around inside her, constantly tossing images of the sexiest bear shifter in the world into her head.

But first, how to deal with her sweetly nosy sister.

"Spill about what?" Her voice was as casual as she could make it, but Alina the hairdresser had been hearing secrets told or kept for years. The woman knew full well when people in her chair were being truthful or not.

"Spill about why you're glowing."

Irritated or not, Brynna couldn't help a small smile as she thought about Wyatt. Behind her, Alina made a little noise in her throat and shook her head, which Brynna caught in the mirror as she looked up. "I knew it. You've got that dreamy little smile you always used to get when you talked about him. Oh, this is so wonderful," she said more softly, her face suddenly serene. "I've always known he was the one for you, Bryn."

Brynna swallowed hard and said nothing. For long moments, there was no sound in the little shop except the sound of cars driving by outside, the Christmas music coming from the speakers, and the soft snip and swish of Alina's scissors.

Mate, the voice inside her insisted. Her reindeer. The little voice always with her, always reminding her she was a reindeer shifter, no matter how far she tried to run from it. And that her reindeer side knew the other truth, no matter how hard she wanted to run away from it.

Wyatt is my mate.

"Fine," Brynna finally, slowly conceded, feeling a sweet little flush even as she said it. "You're right, Ali. Wyatt is—he's the same he always was. And I still love him. So much," she breathed, her voice getting all choked up in her throat as she said it. "Oh, my gosh," she whispered as a flood of emotion roared through her. "I still love him, so much."

She'd never stopped loving him. She'd just run away from it, as far and as fast as she could, because she'd been such a fool. Terrified he would hold her back, just like she'd always been terrified this town and her shifter heritage would hold her back.

Wyatt had never held her back. He'd let her run away from him, break his heart—she knew that as surely as she knew anything—and hadn't tried to stop her. He wanted her to be happy, and he'd let her go to try and find the happiness she thought she wanted.

She'd been wrong. What she wanted in order to be happy, what she *needed* in order to be happy, was Wyatt. Her mate.

Alina grinned hugely in the mirror even as she paid careful attention to her trim job. But her voice was soft when she answered. "I know. I've always known. But you needed to realize it yourself."

Brynna sighed, tapping her fingers on the arm of the chair under the plastic sheet Alina had clipped around her neck. "I think I really knew because...because my reindeer won't shut up about him."

Alina squealed with delight at the same time Brynna's reindeer indignantly huffed inside her mind. Despite herself, Brynna laughed. "I've been feeling her more and more each day I've been back home. Back here in Deep Hollow, I mean," she quickly corrected herself, but Alina had caught it.

Home.

In the mirror, her sister's face softened. "Oh, baby girl, it's not that terrible here, is it? Even though I know you can't wait to leave again."

Brynna watched dark strands of her hair drop onto the plastic sheet and slide down as Alina neatly sliced away with her scissors. She sighed and shrugged. "You know why."

Alina finished the trim and put the scissors into a little container on the counter under the mirror. "It's only one night a year, Bryn. It's not that bad. And it's fun. It's really, really fun."

"Hmm," Brynna murmured. "But you've always liked being a reindeer. Why should I have to be part of holidays I hate, when I never even signed up for being a shifter?"

Alina's eyebrows knotted up. She shook her

head. "No one ever forced you. It's just—it's tradition, Bryn. That's all. And there aren't that many of us in the world, you know," she added, meeting Brynna's eyes in the mirror and holding the gaze. "It's a pretty cool responsibility. A tradition that's loved by many people around the world. And I don't believe you really hate Christmas. I think you've just never given yourself the chance to really love it like you could."

Before Brynna could reply to that, her phone abruptly belted out its jolting ringtone. Alina jumped a bit, then looked down at it. Eyebrows raising and her mouth making a little circle of appreciation, she smiled at it.

"What?" Brynna demanded, twisting around in her chair to reach for her phone.

Her sister smiled, suddenly looking more like a crafty vixen than an innocent reindeer. "If I wasn't head over heels for Thor, I could find Wyatt pretty attractive." She chortled as she looked for her broom to start sweeping up Brynna's hair from the floor, smiling with such a knowing expression that Brynna gritted her teeth.

Fine, so Wyatt was hotter than hot. She stared down at the screen, where his wildly sexy face stared back up at her as he called. At their

CHRISTMAS NIGHT BEAR: WYATT

impromptu dinner, she'd snapped his photo to put in her phone along with his number.

So he looked totally lickable. So just looking at his face made her stomach quiver with butterflies, made her lady bits quiver and clench, too. It just meant she could admit he was crazy hot. Nothing more than that.

Mate, her reindeer insisted.

Well, yes. That too. Yes, he was her mate.

And, I still love him, her own words echoed in her mind.

She slowly exhaled, staring at his smiling face on her phone as it rang.

Alina nudged her shoulder with her hand. "Answer that sexy man before it goes to voicemail. Don't lose this chance, little deer. He still loves you too, you know."

Brynna took a deep breath, then pressed the screen. "Wyatt—" was all she got out before his booming voice came through loudly enough that both she and Alina startled like, well, deer.

"Brynna, where are you? I have to see you. Now." His voice, edged with a molten promise that boomed through the small, thankfully empty salon, seemed to thunder through Brynna's entire body. "Please," he added so softly, so gently, that

she almost dropped the phone. Did he sound
—nervous?

Nervous? Wyatt Walker Webber, fearless
deputy, growly possessive bear, was nervous?
About calling her? About wanting to see her?

She had to swallow a few times, wetting her dry
lips, before she could answer. "I'm getting my hair
cut at Alina's hairdresser shop."

"Okay. I'm on my way. I'll explain everything
when I see you. Just—don't leave, Bryn. Not just
because I don't want you to leave. I want you to do
and be whatever it is you want to be. But don't
leave before I get a chance to tell you what I need
to. " His voice suddenly turned gruff. "Besides, I
have a Christmas gift for you. I'm hoping you'll
like it. Wait for me," he commanded, then hung up.

Brynna sat with her mouth dropped open and
her body shivering with something that might be
delighted hope. Such intense protectiveness had
filled Wyatt's rough voice that her already hitching
breathing hitched even more. Instead of being
pissed, was she suddenly getting all girlishly
turned on because he was acting like such a big,
possessive bear?

Well, yes. Yes, she was.

The strains of "All I Want for Christmas is You"

gently echoed around the room as Alina, her eyes shining, met Brynna's gaze in the mirror. "He's running right to you this time. Don't run away from him again, Bryn. That big ole bear of a man will have another broken heart he'll never recover from this time. And so will you," her sister added in a whisper. "You know shifters need their mates, or you'll never be really happy or fulfilled. Besides, he's bringing you a Christmas gift. Wait to see what it is. And," Alina tapped the side of her nose as she gave Brynna a thoughtful look, "I have an idea. Something I think might make everything work out the way it always should have."

Brynna's entire body trembled as she nodded. Okay. Yes. She wasn't going anywhere just yet. She would listen to Alina's idea. She would wait for Wyatt.

My mate, her heart sang, sending another flood of wild joy surging through her. Her mate was coming for her, finally. Her entire body sizzled with nerves and a blast of giddy excitement.

Home, her reindeer whispered firmly.

Yes. Yes, she just might be home.

6

Wyatt pounded along the snowy sidewalk, half-running from around the block where he'd parked his truck on the other end of town from the sheriff's station. He drew more than a few stares but he didn't care. He had to find Brynna right now, no matter what. His bear roamed around inside him, barely restrained beneath the surface. He had to get to her. Had to see her. His sweet, sexy, stubborn little reindeer mate.

Ducking and dodging passersby, he headed straight toward Alina's shop, which of course he remembered from before he'd moved away. Alina had always liked to mess with people's hair and had opened her little place only a few years after they all graduated from high school. The pretty storefront window proclaimed ALINA'S HAIR DESIGN, with a fancy pair of scissors painted onto the sign below the name. Reaching forward, Wyatt yanked open the door, then lunged inside, quickly skidding to a stop on the slick floor.

Brynna sat in a chair in front of a mirror, swiveled around to face the door, her dark hair floating in loose, pretty waves around her face, her eyes wide as she stared at him. Her sister Alina stood beside her, holding a hair dryer, wearing a beaming smile.

Suddenly feeling like a reactive idiot, Wyatt took one more step toward Brynna before he stopped, his heart racing. "Uh...hi."

"Hi." Brynna's voice was tentative, but not angry. Thank fuck.

He scrubbed a quick hand over his eyes. He needed to focus. He couldn't screw this up again. Never again. Taking a breath, he reached out and gently laid his hands on top of Brynna's shoulders, leaning forward to look directly into her eyes. She shivered slightly under his touch, but it was an appreciative shiver. Touching her felt right. "I want to talk to you, Brynna. Seeing you again the other night was—I don't know. A sign, maybe.

Then again yesterday. Almost like it was meant to be."

Feeling somewhat ridiculous as he said that, he searched her face for any trace she was laughing at him. She just nodded, looking as serious as he suddenly felt.

His heart thumped hard at how beautiful she was. At just how *Brynna* she was.

"And you're still here. You haven't left yet. But," he gave a quick glance at Alina, who was still smiling at him as if he were some sort of rare object of which she clearly approved, "could we talk in private? If that's okay with you."

He suddenly felt tentative. She had been pissed at him for being so domineering the other night, then such a jackass with Thor yesterday morning. Who, he abruptly recalled, was Alina's fiance. Feeling a little embarrassed for what a possessive jerk he'd been, for how snarly he'd been with Brynna's sister's mate, he shot another glance at Alina. But she still smiled at him. Clearly, if she knew about that incident, she didn't care about it.

There was silence in the small shop as Brynna looked at him even longer. Shit. He'd pushed too hard earlier, with his over-the-top protectiveness, and she wasn't going to listen. Could he really blame her? But to his relief, she finally nodded.

"I'll go with you and listen to whatever it is you have to tell me." Her face softened. "I have something to tell you too. A few somethings, actually."

He let out a breath he hadn't even realized he'd been holding. "Okay. Let's go. I'm taking you to my place."

Alina whooped. "About time!"

Brynna smiled as she stood up, about stopping his heart with her beauty. "Let's go," she said, looking at Wyatt and holding out her hand. "I'm ready."

Wyatt took her hand, feeling the softness of her skin yet the strength of her fingers. His Brynna had two sides like that. Yes, *his* Brynna, no matter what. As long as she was cool with it too. He sure as hell hoped so. This time, he swore to himself, he'd better not fuck it up again by acting like a damned he-man who wanted to throw his mate over his shoulder and march off to his bear cave with her.

Even if he did.

On the short drive through the snowy streets to his house, they were silent. Brynna stared out the window, obviously thinking about everything. But he caught a smile on her pretty mouth more than once.

When they got to Wyatt's place, Brynna didn't say anything for a long moment. She just sat examining the small house as he killed the engine. He'd just barely managed to put a down payment on it with what he'd saved from a deputy's slim salary over the past several years, but the place was his. Feeling suddenly self-conscious, Wyatt said in a gruff voice, "I just bought it. I know it's small, but I swear it's pretty decent inside."

She puffed laughter. "Wyatt. I'm not worried about the inside. The outside looks you invited Christmas over for a visit, and it decided to completely take over."

Oh. That. "Well, you know me." He sat back and tried to look at his house the way Brynna must be seeing it. Yeah, he hadn't been shy about decorating his place the second he'd moved in. He didn't think it was completely over the top. But it was definitely filled with holiday spirit.

His snug little house in the middle of town was covered in twinkling lights. Colorful outside lights and white ones that blinked from inside where he'd carefully draped them around the windows. Gaudy plastic reindeers, enormous fake snowmen, and a cheerful Santa decorated—desecrated, he'd bet Brynna was thinking to herself—his snow-covered front yard. A smiling elf head bobbed out from his mailbox on the street. His tree, which he'd brought down from the mountain himself on a tree-getting mission with Slade and his other cousins, presented itself in the front window. It glowed with lights, which were set with a timer to come on before dusk.

Yeah, he was a holiday-loving guy once more, and that was that.

He glanced at Brynna again. Christmas might be her least favorite holiday, but she knew he loved it. He couldn't and wouldn't hide that from her. To his relief, a smile played on her face. She glanced over at him. "Well, some things definitely don't change. Now," she said, opening her door to get out. "Let me see the inside."

Frantically, he sifted through his memories of the morning, trying to decide whether or not he'd left the place a pigsty. He decided it probably wasn't too bad, as long as he kept her away from the kitchen. Another grin tip-toed onto her face as she got out of the truck and went up to the front door, then stopped to wait for him. He opened the door and somewhat shyly gestured for her to go inside.

Damn. This suddenly felt like a really big deal. He'd bought a house of his own. This was his personal bear cave, so to speak. The need for Brynna to like it seemed wildly important all of a sudden.

When they stepped inside, she made a cute little startled sound. "Oh! This is nicer than I thought it would be."

"Hmm. What exactly were you picturing?"

Brynna laughed, the sound sending actual fuckin' flutters through Wyatt's body. It was nuts. But he liked it. "Well, I know you, so I figured it would be practically empty except for maybe a beanbag chair and some pizza boxes." She shot him a side-eye look, an even bigger grin sneaking onto her face.

Wyatt snorted, relaxing into the familiar repartee. This was the Brynna from dinner the other night. The Brynna he'd known years ago. "I'm not a frat boy. I've grown up some since I was last here."

She gave him a probing look, as if trying to see his grown-up side. Then she just nodded, her hair flowing prettily over her shoulders as she looked around. She turned in a slow circle, taking in the place in all its holiday glory. When she finally had spun all the way around to face him again, her eyes studied him for another long moment, leaving Wyatt felt stripped bare. It was unsettling and exciting at the same time. He wanted her to know him. He wanted her to *see* him. The real him that she used to know. Apparently, so did she, based on her next words.

"Wyatt, tell me why I'm here with you right now." Her voice wobbled for a brief moment, but she didn't break her eye contact with him. "And then I'll tell you why I never should have left."

7

Brynna studied Wyatt as he stared at her, her heart hammering in her chest so loudly she was half surprised he couldn't hear it. The bright, naked hope that sprang into his expression told her everything. He did want her to stay. And everything in her—especially her pushy little reindeer, she thought, almost giggling at the irritated huffs that blew around her mind—wanted him to give her the right reason she should.

Wyatt's mouth ticked up at the corners. A smile. "I've always been able to tell you everything, Bryn." The low rumble of his voice sent a heated flicker through her core, thrumming along her nerves in all the right ways. Despite her roller coaster emotions about him, she'd been aroused ever since he burst into Alina's shop like a sexy warrior, ready to claim his woman.

"You remember I told you what it was like to grow up without a mom. To see what it did to my dad. To be one of the only shifter kids in town without a mom." He watched her carefully as he said that. They had touched on it during their stroll after dinner last week, but they hadn't discussed this part quite so boldly.

Brynna nodded, feeling held by the intensity of his bright blue eyes. Just as carefully but very clearly, she responded. "Yes. And how her leaving tore apart your family, and made your dad the way he is. Made you the way you are," she added more hesitantly.

Wyatt visibly shut his mouth on whatever words he had been planning to say. He crinkled up his face at her. "The way I am? How am I?"

She paused, assessing him. He could take it, she decided. Lying to Wyatt, even by omission, wasn't something she'd ever want to do anyway. For some reason, she couldn't bring herself to ever be false to him.

"You," she started slowly, dragging out the word as his brilliant eyes seemed to try to pierce into her soul, "are guarded, too. You never really shared all of yourself with me, you know. Not even when you planned to ask me to marry you." He flinched at that, hard, but she pressed on. She had to. "I know we told each other everything, but you held back on me."

He drew breath to speak, his brows lowering, but she shook her head and went on more quickly. "No, hear me out. I don't believe you ever lied to me about anything, Wyatt. Never," she said as firmly as she could. He relaxed a fraction. "But," and he tensed again, "you weren't completely there. Not really. You trusted me with your secrets, but not everything. I could still tell that, at dinner the other night. What is it that you're still not telling me, Wyatt? I think that after we somehow came back into each other's lives, after all this time, I deserve to hear it all."

Holding her breath, she waited. But it seemed Wyatt hadn't been law enforcement for years, not to mention a boy who'd grown up with a man who didn't show much affection or emotion over anything, to not have learned things. Instead of telling her, he neatly turned the tables on her.

"Tell me first," he said in an equally careful yet firm voice, "about what you saw that night that made you run away from me. The real reason."

Darn it. She fidgeted under his unwavering blue stare. He'd called her several times after their unexpected dinner date and kiss the other night, asking what had happened. Texted her, too. She'd hung onto her annoyance that he'd lunged after that random guy who'd wandered too close and stared at her too long, using it as an excuse to not call him back.

But now she could no longer hide behind the excuse of his temper being the reason to not tell him the truth. Taking a breath, she walked over to the window of his living room. It looked out onto the street, where more snowflakes were just beginning to fall. Up and down the cute little street, Christmas lights twinkled merrily from snug little houses just like this one.

Turning back around from the window, she looked at Wyatt. "I've never been happy being a reindeer shifter. You've always known that."

He nodded, his eyes shadowing.

"The expectations on us, they always made me kind of crazy. I mean, in concept, it's so sweet. But in reality? I hated having been born to something that I'd never asked for." She always struggled to describe it. Everyone else thought being a reindeer shifter was so cool. Especially this time of year.

"I know." Wyatt's voice was as soft as Brynna's. "I remember hiding out on Christmas Eve with you so many times growing up. I think my dad whupped my butt a few times because we got the whole town riled up, out looking for you. And I was the one hiding you."

She couldn't stop the huge smile that burst out for his acknowledgement that he remembered just as much of what she had said as she did about him.

Holding his gaze, she continued. "Standing on the riverwalk with you the other night, feeling you touch me, hold me, kiss me, it all just felt—so right. So right, Wyatt." She could hear her voice going kind of dreamy as she replayed what happened that night, but kept her gaze firmly locked with his. "The breeze, the moonlight, the smell of you."

His mouth quirked and he raised an eyebrow. She let a slow, appreciative smile unfurl on her lips.

"Your scent is of deep forests and big ancient trees. Like the wild night itself." Just describing his scent, which naturally she could smell right this moment, Brynna felt shivers whispering over her skin. Wyatt's eyes darkened even more.

"It all blended, and intensified. It felt like when we were together before. And I knew you had just moved back here, and you got this great job, and you bought a house, and you were happy. And for just a moment, it felt like maybe I'd made a mistake before. Leaving you five years ago, when you tried to give me that ring. And I said no." She couldn't stop the shake in her voice. Shame, sadness, loss. It suddenly felt almost over-whelming.

He stood unmoving, but listening intently.

"And then I was standing there with you, wrapped in your arms, being kissed just like you always used to kiss me before—"

Wyatt's scent deepened into something wild and hot that was beginning to make her dizzy. In a very good way.

"—and then suddenly I just knew what was going to happen." She paused to swallow hard before going on. "You were going to lead me to your home, to this place actually, and take me to bed. It was going to blow my socks off." She could hear her own voice dropping as she spoke, could feel the delicious chills of anticipation billowing through her now even as she shared her vision of what should have happened but that she had stopped so that it would never exist. Her and Wyatt, together. Happy in a little house with a picket fence, maybe a dog, living in a little town that had expectations of her.

"I could practically see every single second of it. Then I imagined that you would bite me. On my neck. That you would claim me, without asking me first. And I got so mad at that thought, the thought of someone trying to control me yet again, like being a reindeer shifter has controlled me all my life, that I just got pissed. And then you almost went after that guy that night." She jerked her shoulders in a shrug. "It made me so angry, Wyatt."

Swallowing a few times against her suddenly dry throat, she went on. "I know we're mates. I know we are. But—" She broke off, because saying out loud to Wyatt the things she'd already acknowledged to herself was pretty damned hard.

Wyatt spoke, his voice low and gravelly and brimming with the molten heat. That, and an emotion she couldn't quite pinpoint. "Tell me."

She took a deep, shuddering breath. She blinked once but still didn't take her gaze from him. "I never wanted to be a shifter, but I was one. And you were my mate. And it made me so angry to not have a choice about that, like I didn't have a choice about being a reindeer shifter, that I just decided to run away. Because I was too terrified of facing the truth. I was too darned young, Wyatt. I didn't really understand what I was letting go of."

She looked right at him as she said all that. He just looked right back at her, holding her gaze but letting her speak without interrupting.

Her voice barely above a whisper, she added, "I knew you were going to propose that night. Slade let it slip that he went ring shopping with you weeks before. Between that and my family getting so mad at me again, on Christmas Eve, that I just didn't want to be a fucking reindeer shifter pulling a damned sleigh all night long, that I panicked. I found the job in Florida, and left."

She'd felt almost smothered, and the only thing she could do was run away.

"I just pulled away and ran from you. I'm so sorry I did that," she whispered, meaning it with every part of her. "Wyatt, I'm so sorry I ran. I never should have left."

Wyatt shook his head, his eyes suddenly shining something more than just his bear. "I'm the one who's fucking sorry. I never should have let you go. I should have gone after you and told you we could handle anything, as long as we were together. But I panicked too. So I didn't go after you, but I should have. Because you're my home, and I'm yours."

The words rolled through her with unshake-able certainty, settling deep into her very bones. Into her soul.

She took a step toward him, but he held up a hand. Puzzled, she stopped.

"Bryn, we still have to talk about one more thing."

She swallowed hard, her gaze on his so unblinking her eyes were starting to feel dry.

He took a deep breath, and she suddenly real-ized he was just as nervous as she was. "You love your job. I know that. And you're good at it. You told me as much the other night at dinner."

Yes. She did love her job, and she was good at it.

"I would never keep you from that. So," he took a deep breath, "I'm giving my notice at the sheriff's department. I know Miami doesn't have deputies, they have cops, but I could be a cop. I'm qualified."

He stopped talking, though he didn't look away from her. Brynna finally blinked, because now tears were beginning to well in her eyes. "You— you'd leave Deep Hollow? For me?" Her voice cracked. "But you love it here, Wyatt. And you would hate Miami. You've never liked big cities."

The corner of Wyatt's mouth turned up in a rueful smile as he shook his head. "No, I don't like big cities at all. Too many people. But that doesn't matter. You would be there. And you're all I need. Wherever you are is my home now, Brynna Darby. I mean that."

Holy shit, open the floodgates. Tears tumbled down her cheeks as she stared at him. He groaned, almost moving toward her, but he stayed put. "Tell me you want me to go with you. I won't do it unless you really want me there." His voice roughened with intensity. "This time, we're making sure that we're each honoring what the other wants."

Shaking her head, Brynna choked out, "N-no way, Wyatt Webber. I'd never want you to live somewhere you hate. You wouldn't be happy there, even with me."

His eyes darkened. "I'll be happy anywhere in the world with you."

A smile pushed its way through her tears. Wyatt's eyes darkened even more, but she quickly said, "Hold on. My brilliant sister came up with a plan. One I think is perfect. Wyatt," and now it was her turn to take a deep breath, "I'm staying in Deep Hollow. With you."

He rocked back on his feet. "What? No. You hate it here more than I'd hate Miami." Despite his words, she saw the hope flaring in him.

Her tears retreated as her smile grew. "No. That was never really true, though I thought it was. I hated feeling controlled here. Constricted. But that was *my* issue. It was never Deep Hollow's fault. And I've realized it now. Deep Hollow never held me back, and neither did you." She made a regretful sound and shrugged. "I did that all to myself, and I realize that now. So here's how I can stay here with you but still be true to what I want and need."

Her sexy bear looked at her, his entire heart in his eyes as he waited for what she had to say.

She took another deep breath, her heart hammering. "If my company will let me, I'll live here and travel to their offices a few times a year, but otherwise I can fly out from Durango to still do tours." Deep Hollow was too small to have its own airport, but luckily Durango wasn't that far away. "And I won't do as many, but that's okay with me. Honestly, I was getting a little tired of nonstop travel. I wouldn't mind slowing down some."

Wyatt's expression was guarded yet wildly hopeful. "Will they let you do that?"

Now Brynna's smile exploded over her face as she told him the best part of what Alina had thought up. "I hope so, because they're a good company to work for. But if not, it's still okay. Because I have so much experience now, and so many good contacts all over the world, I could start my own global guiding company from right here in Deep Hollow. A small one, but a solid one. I don't need clients to come to my office, I'd just meet them at whichever destination anywhere on the planet. Everything is planned online and by phone. I could do it, Wyatt," she whispered. "I'd do anything to be with you and to keep us both happy. Happy together, here. At home."

Silence ticked through the room for long moments as he stared at her and she stared right back at him. His eyes glowed bright with his bear, his face open and vulnerable as he took in what she'd said. Finally, slowly, a smile matching hers spread over his face.

"Your sister is smart." His voice rumbled

through the room, setting her nerves on delicious fire.

"She is." Her words came out breathy as her heart still walloped inside her.

"Well then. I guess it's true that mates will always find a way to be together eventually." Wyatt's eyes blazed on hers as he said that.

"Yes." Brynna's voice was a whisper by now.

He added in a low voice that was almost rough with its certainty, "I know something else that's true, Bryn."

The zap of electric tension sizzled between them, making her skin tingle.

"You're my mate. I know that to the center of my being. We both do. Since you're staying here and we're going to be together, there's one more thing I know for sure."

She swallowed at the sudden, sweet hunger on his face. "What's that?" she whispered, her voice rattling in her throat with a building excitement.

He took a short step toward her. Close enough that she could almost feel the heat radiating off his body.

"That you, my beautiful little deer," he closed the last bit of distance between them, "really do want me to bite you and claim you as mine. Don't you?" he whispered, the heat of his body right on hers, making her skin hum with desire. "That's the gift I have for you. My Christmas gift to you. But only," he added fiercely, "only if you want it. I would never take that without asking you, Bryn."

Her knees shook as she nodded, joy exploding through her entire body. "Yes, Wyatt," she whispered. "Yes. That's exactly what I want. I'll never, ever run from you again. Claim me as yours. Claim me as your mate."

He caught her chin in his big hand, tipped her head back, and kissed her like a drowning man who'd just found salvation.

8

Everything in Brynna's body hummed with a deep knowing that this was right. That this was what she wanted. Oh, this man. This sexy, hot, strong bear shifter. All hers. He pulled back, looking at her hard, a question in his eyes.

Still mesmerized by his brilliant gaze, dazed by the kiss she could feel all throughout her body, she silently nodded. Without another word, Wyatt growled, reached forward, and scooped her up in his strong arms. She couldn't stop her startled squeak. Geez, what a girl she was being.

Geez, how she didn't care about that right now.

Holding her tightly to his chest, he took swift steps toward his large bed. Gently setting her down, he stepped back to look down at her in sheer worship. "You're the most beautiful woman I have ever seen in my life, Brynna. Inside and out." He said the words with such truthful devotion that all girlish squeals died in her throat as she stared up at him with wide eyes.

Without even a moment's hesitation, he added into the hush, "I'm going to show you right now how beautiful you are. Every single inch of you. I've been dying to do this ever since our last kiss."

Brynna gaped at him, feeling the warm hum of anticipation skitter through her entire body. In her head, she flashed right on the images of exactly what he probably was going to do to her. Do with her. And what she would do with him. The decadent thoughts made her blush so hard in mingled excitement and awe that Wyatt's sensual mouth curved into a grin. "Oh, yeah," he murmured.

Oh, yeah, was right. This was exactly what she wanted right now.

"Come here to me." She reached her arms up to him as excitement shivered through her.

"As you wish." His grin now edged with a feral arousal, her wild, sexy Wyatt quickly obeyed her. The bed creaked slightly as he settled onto it, his weight a welcome feeling against her every nerve ending.

"Too many clothes. Off now." His voice was a focused mutter as he reached down to tug off her shirt, then help her shimmy out of her jeans.

She helped him as much as she could, wiggling and shifting and lifting her butt off the bed. When he momentarily lost his concentration as she thrust her hips up off the bed, it was so flat out sexy her breath caught in her throat.

Wyatt was her man. Her bear.

Her mate.

Or not quite yet. For that to happen, he had to officially claim her. Just the thought of that, of what it meant, sent pleasure skittering up and down her spine, radiating out through her limbs in tingles. All that mattered was that she wanted to connect with him. Right now, in every way possible.

She'd thought about this moment off and on for years, subconsciously using Wyatt as the perfect fantasy man to whom no others could hold a candle. She could admit it now. Especially now. The breathless reality of the moment was even more thrilling than she'd ever imagined possible.

"I've pictured this for a long time." Wyatt's voice crackled with desire. "It's shaping up to be even better than I ever dreamed."

Brynna's entire body felt alive as she watched the sexy man above her quickly stripping off his clothes. "I was literally just thinking the same thing. I guess that means it was fated to be." She said the last part somewhat teasingly, lips curved into a smile. But Wyatt's expression turned serious, although it didn't lose any of the hunger.

"Yes." His voice was slightly hoarse. "I never thought it could be, but yes."

She felt a ripple of something deep and powerful inside her as he said that. It was like every cell in her body yearned toward him, urging her to get close to him. "Hurry, love." Her voice also edged into a low hoarseness as she lifted her arms to him.

He wasted no time, kicking off his pants and surging toward her.

"Wait. Wow." She wanted to enjoy this first moment of seeing him naked again in years. It was like looking at the most perfect male specimen ever. Every muscle in his body was chiseled, from washboard abs to muscular thighs. But the most important, most exciting thing to her, was that he was Wyatt. Her Wyatt. Knowing she was with him turned her on more than she ever had been in her life.

He stood still for her inspection for mere moments before shaking his head. "Enough. If I don't touch you right now I might explode." With that, he closed the last distance to her on the bed, half nestling with her and half hovering over her, supporting his upper body on his forearms.

"Gotta kiss you again," he said so softly it felt like butterfly wings across her skin.

He did exactly that, his mouth taking hers with a strength that was as tender as it was fierce, as wondering and exploring as it was also familiar. It was as if they'd been doing this their whole lives, yet it was also so stunningly new that Brynna shivered. Wyatt abruptly broke off the kiss, pulling back to study her.

"Is this okay? Am I being too rough?" He sounded genuinely concerned, but she sensed the longing as well.

She shook her head, lifting a hand to touch his face. "No," she whispered. "I love it. Kiss me again. Everywhere."

With a groan, he complied. His long, hard body stretched out on top of hers, sinking onto her more. He fisted one hand in her hair, gently holding her head on the pillow. His other hand cupped the side of her face and neck. He kissed her so long, so deep, it seemed as if she could feel their souls joining already.

"You taste incredible," he murmured against her face, turning his head to kiss his way down her cheekbone.

She pushed her head into the pillow, running one hand along his back as his lips traveled to her collarbone, then down one breast. He caught the nipple between his lips, sucking and gently biting, then moved to the other one. She cried out, pushing her breasts into his mouth and shame-lessly shoving her pelvis against his. Lightly moving his mouth on her softness, his tongue came out to swirl around the rock hard nipples, back and forth from one to the other.

"Wyatt," she gasped, the sound of it bouncing around the little room.

In answer, he gently disentangled his other hand from her hair and brushed it down her side, stroking down her ribs, curving over her breast. Then he spread his fingers across her soft belly, stroking her. Slowly, he moved his hand down, then let a finger travel to explore her soft, wet center. Brynna cried out as he gently pushed one thick, broad digit inside, gently swirling around in her wetness.

"I've been dreaming about this nonstop for the past week. Hell, for the past five years." His voice vibrated through her body.

Feeling half dazed by the building ecstasy, she just nodded. Driven by some deep, primal urging she didn't understand but felt was right, she leaned forward to kiss him, hard, at the spot where his neck met his shoulder. He sharply inhaled, the vibration from it seeming to rattle down his spine beneath her fingertips.

"Inside," she commanded in a low gasp, more sure of this than anything in her life. "I want you inside me, Wyatt. Now."

9

I *want you inside me, Wyatt. Now.* The words seemed to hang in the room, their sweet invitation wrapping around Wyatt's brain and causing it to stop working. All he was right now was pure sensation, pure joy and rightness with Brynna.

His Brynna. His mate.

"Whatever you want," he managed to say, his voice ragged. His cock throbbed, eager to be inside her. He'd been almost painfully hard for the last fifteen minutes.

His fingers told him she was ready. The soft moan deep in her throat, the way her eyes fixed on his with an intensity that seemed to connect them together, told him she wanted this just as much. She rolled her thighs apart, tipping her hips up at him again. He groaned, feeling the fire roar through him. Feeling his bear push at him to claim his mate, to bite her slender neck, to make her his. Her beautiful breasts, bare and soft and still glistening from where his mouth had feasted, moved up and down from the tempo of her breathing. Reaching up, he pulled her arms over her head and clasped her wrists in his hands, gently holding them to the pillow.

Brynna smiled up at him, her pulse banging in her neck as her spicy-sweet scent rose in waves, almost overpowering him with lust. "Now," she said again, her voice half-command, half-laugh, and all strong, sexy woman. Then, "Fucking right now, Wyatt," she whispered in a ragged cry, all play gone from her face. Her voice shook, her body shook.

He thought his soul shook, too.

"Yes. Now," he whispered back. Spreading his weight on his knees between her open legs, he thrust his aching cock inside her.

Wyatt almost roared with the stunning explosion of tight heat, with the way Brynna's mouth fell open as she panted. She tilted her hips up more, to accommodate him. He slid inside, eliciting a small gasp from her as he pushed against the tightness.

"I'm sorry." Her voice bumped as his thrust slid her over the sheets. "It's been a while."

Wyatt stopped, making her cry out a soft, "No, don't stop!"

"I don't want to hear about anyone else ever again," he growled, tipping his head down to lightly nip at her ear, then her shoulder. "Just me."

"Same back to you," she retorted, though a sweet moan underscored her voice.

Wyatt pulled his head back to look at her. Brynna's gaze was clear, even though her face was soft with her need. He nodded. "Deal," he said in a low voice, before he abruptly thrust all the way inside her.

She gasped and arched her head back, meeting his strokes by pushing up toward him. Letting him fill her completely, the sweet moans coming from her lips telling him how much she liked having him there. He increased the rate, changed the angle, and never stopped the delicious slip and slide and thrust of this most ancient dance.

Fucking hell, but doing this with Brynna was the singular most amazing experience of Wyatt's life.

"Wyatt," she gasped, low and throaty, her eyes wide on his as her hands pressed hard onto his back. "More. Don't stop. I'm close," she said in a ragged warble. "I want to be looking at you when I come."

He just nodded, keeping his eyes on hers, diving again and again into her soft heat. He felt his own orgasm spiraling up through him as hers began to rise as well, judging by how her pupils got bigger and her moans got faster and her hands clutched him tighter, fingers digging deep into his flesh as she hung on to him.

"Wyatt," she said again, looking directly at him. Then she tilted her head to the side, exposing her neck. "Claim me." Her ragged voice trembled with the force of her need.

"Bryn," he growled. "Yes."

Crackles of blinding hot lightning seemed to fill his every cell as he reached forward, plunging his sharp teeth into the sweet spot between her shoulder and collarbone. They pierced her skin as he claimed his mate. He tasted the sweet ambrosia that was Brynna on his tongue. Then he roared as an orgasm blasted through him, so intense he thought he might black out.

Brynna screamed, her face blazing with ecstasy. Joy exploded out from her, surrounding them both as Wyatt was held inside her, her walls pulsing around his shaft as he spilled his seed into her, spilled his own cry into the room to mingle with hers. They rose in ecstasy together, billowing waves of pleasure holding them together, the feeling so stunning that Wyatt thought his head might blow off from the joy of it.

Brynna. His mate. His soul.

Slowly, bit by bit, the head-banging sensations lessened, gradually ebbing away. Very slowly, very gently, they eventually collapsed into a tangle of sated bodies onto the soft bed. Wyatt carefully lowered himself on top of her, half off to the side, holding her close to him. Her sweaty skin beneath his, her intoxicating scent filling him, were his entire world as every other thought still stayed far away.

"Wyatt," she said long moments later in soft, lazy voice, the sound already edging toward sleepy.

He chuckled, masculine pride rearing up in him even as he fought his own satisfied yawn. He meant to say, "So it was good, huh?" but instead he somehow whispered, "I love you, babe. Always have."

His beautiful mate murmured back a sleepy "Mmm," snuggling into him and letting him hold her tight. Then she pulled back a bit, looking him in the eyes, and quietly said, "I love you too, Wyatt. I always have."

Brynna had a sappy expression on her face that Wyatt was pretty sure matched his own.

He broke the silence by saying, "My tiny little deer. As always."

"You—you—" she sputtered, though her smile was still huge.

"Big cave bear," he suggested, grinning back at her.

She threw her head back and laughed, a pure, joyous sound that echoed through him. "Home." She breathed the word. "I really am home, Wyatt." Her voice was soft but the words rang through the quiet room. "This really, truly is exactly where I'm supposed to be."

He held his mate close, breathing in her scent.

An enormous smile blazed over her face. "It finally feels so right to be here. With you."

Fierce joy swept him again as he caught her up tight in his arms, kissed her gorgeous lips until they both gasped for breath, laughing together in his bed.

Together with his mate, right where they both belonged.

Her face was almost obliterated by another

yawn. Wyatt grinned into her hair, taking a deep inhale to smell her and sighing back with contentment. "My Bryn," he said in wonder, gently stroking her back. "You're my home, too, now and forever. Merry Christmas Eve, mate," he added, nuzzling her hair and kissing her ear.

"Mm-hmm. Merry Christmas Eve to you too, World Wide Web. Sleep now, mate," she murmured against his chin, her entire body relaxed as she drifted off in his arms.

Holding her close, Wyatt did just that.

EPILOGUE

Brynna drifted up from a deep sleep when her phone went off with a text notification. Strangely enough, it sounded like sleigh bells jingling, which was not the text tone she'd set. Fumbling for it, smiling sleepily as Wyatt exhaled and turned over beside her, she blinked until her eyes came into focus. Who the heck was texting her this late? On Christmas Eve?

Then she saw the name on her phone and all the air whooshed out of her.

ST. NICK, it read.

No. No way. She'd taken good old Saint Nick's number out of her phone years ago, when she'd left Deep Hollow. But apparently Christmas magic worked like this. His number was right back in her phone, with the same jingle bell ringtone it used to have.

Her phone softly jingled again. *Glad you finally came home, little deer. Come on outside. I have a business proposition for you.*

A business proposition?

Jingle jingle. *Just need you to sign some paperwork first. There's room for that bear of yours too. He seems to really enjoy the holiday spirit. Hurry up, the others are out here with me and they're getting impatient.*

Room for her bear? Paperwork? The others? Brynna stared at her phone, her brain still foggy.

Lots of kids waiting for their gifts, Brynna. We only have one night to get them all out there. Put a hustle in your step.

Blinking, Brynna automatically sat up. Old habits died hard. She couldn't say no to the old man, even though she'd shaken her fist at his hold on her life ever since she had learned what being a rare reindeer shifter was all about. Truthfully, she was happy to see him again. She had to admit she'd missed his cheerful presence.

Pausing, she looked back at Wyatt snoozing so peacefully beside her. Her gorgeous, sexy, amazing mate. Leaning down, she whispered a bare kiss onto his shoulder. He murmured in his sleep, making her smile. Then she swung her feet out of the warm bed.

Quietly, Brynna dressed and tiptoed out of the house, wincing as a floorboard creaked. She slipped out the front door, carefully shutting it behind her. Walking out almost all the way to the street, she turned around and looked up into the crisp, star-filled sky, searching the rooftops.

Ah. There they were. Right on top of Wyatt's roof, actually.

Shaking her head, Brynna couldn't help smiling. "A sleigh and seven tiny reindeer," she said, rolling her eyes at one female reindeer who giggled quietly. Alina, of course. "You're missing one, you know," she pointed out. "There are supposed to be eight."

Alina snorted and pawed at the roof, jingling the traces.

Brynna looked at the jolly old man dressed in red seated in the sleigh, glasses slipping down his nose as he gently rattled some papers in her direction. Nodding at him, she said, "Okay. Tell me about your business proposition, St. Nick. I'm listening."

Wyatt woke out of a sound sleep with Brynna's sweet voice echoing in his head. He blinked, reaching out a hand to search for her. But no sweet, sleeping mate was to be found. Waking up completely, he realized his phone was ringing. He swatted his hand around the bedside table until he found it, then squinted at the screen.

Brynna was calling. Utterly confused, he answered. "Babe? Where are you?"

Her voice burbled out, giddy with excitement. "Come outside, Wyatt. I've got something really cool to show you. I think you'll love it. Hurry! We're all waiting."

What the hell? "Who's waiting—" he began, but she just laughed and hung up.

Rubbing his hand across his eyes, Wyatt got out of bed. He yanked on a pair of pants and headed outside into the dark, quiet night. Snow covered every yard, the streetlamps cast a golden glow on the ground, and lit trees twinkled out of every house window on the block. But no Brynna.

"Hey, man," a deep, somewhat familiar voice called out from somewhere above him. "Up here."

Wyatt twisted around and looked up. Then his jaw dropped. On the roof of his house sat a sleigh. Leather traces attached it to eight reindeer, each one of which was pawing the roof—his roof, for crying out loud—and snorting or shaking their heads. Impatience was clear in each one.

A sleigh with eight tiny reindeer. Holy shit. Was he dreaming?

Seated in the sleigh was Thor, wearing a frigging Santa outfit. Red velvet hat trimmed in fluffy white, red velvet suit with a shiny black belt, a big old belly, a huge white beard. The whole nine yards. Wyatt's jaw stayed dropped.

Thor waved an impatient arm at him. "Hurry up. These guys are getting really restless. It's hard to hold them back."

A female shifter's voice, speaking in her deer language yet perfectly understandable to Wyatt, crackled out into the cold, magical night. "Thor Calhoun, you'd better know by now you can't hold me back." She sounded surprisingly dainty despite her slightly deeper voice in her shifted form.

Wyatt rubbed his eyes, then looked again. That sounded like Brynna's sister, Alina. He peered hard. Yup, that was her all right, in the traces at the head of the team.

Right beside her, daintily pawing his roof and sending puffs of air out each time she snorted, was the prettiest little deer shifter in the world.

Holy shit once more.

"Brynna?" Wyatt stared, a disbelieving grin finally spreading over his face. He hadn't seen Brynna as her reindeer in forever.

Her little laugh echoed out over the roofs of the houses on Wyatt's street. "It's me!" Her voice sounded so excited, so happy, that a huge smile blazed over Wyatt's face.

"Come on up here, bear." Her cute little face bobbed up and down, her ears wiggling at him. "I signed a deal with Saint Nicholas. He's in charge of all the individual Santas around the world, so he's really busy this time of year. They really did miss having me here."

Wyatt blinked, still smiling. "Uh, come again?"

Brynna's voice giggled with joy. "I'm part of the annual Deep Hollow Christmas Night sleigh team now. It is only once a year, after all. And," Brynna's voice suddenly went a little shy, "there's something else really cool that I think you'll enjoy. Since Alina and Thor are going to try to start making little shifter babies as soon as they're married next year"—Alina deer-giggled while Thor grunted happily—"Thor plans to step down as the local Santa. So, you can be the new Santa in Deep Hollow, Wyatt. If you want it, I mean. I know how much you love Christmas. We all know that."

There was a little pause. Then Brynna whispered in a suspiciously thick voice that trembled right on the edge of happy little reindeer tears, "Merry Christmas, mate. I hope you like my gift to you."

Wyatt felt something suspiciously like tears prickle at his own eyelids. Damn. His Brynna, his mate, knew him so well. She had just made him the happiest bear in town. Probably the happiest one on the entire planet.

Nodding, feeling his face splitting into a crazy huge grin, Wyatt had to swallow and blink hard a few times before he could trust himself to speak. "Yeah, babe. I love it. I'll be Santa on Christmas Eve every year. As long as you keep pulling the sleigh."

Alina burbled, "Awwww!" echoed by the happy little noises of the rest of the reindeer team.

A deep, peaceful silence billowed around them for a moment, broken only by the soft snorts of the reindeer. Wyatt now recognized them all as Brynna's extended family, including her parents. And one little guy at the back, who looked an awful lot like—

"Deputy Donner? Is that you?" Apparently the kid wasn't a rodent shifter after all.

The rookie deputy nodded ecstatically, sending all the bells on the traces to jingling. He even had silver tinsel wound through his antlers. "That's me! I'm Brynna's and Alina's second cousin. And see, I told you we'd be a good team. Either on the patrol beat or on Christmas Eve. Come on, Deputy Webber. It's the most fun ever."

Thor chimed in, as did the team of deer with happy little barks and huffing sounds. "Let's do this, Wyatt! I'll be the lead Santa tonight and show you how it's done. I think you're gonna love it, man. But let's get going. We've got a lot of gifts to deliver. It's starting to snow again, too."

Wyatt's grin got bigger and bigger. Big, beautiful snowflakes had indeed begun to drift down from the sky. Looking at the roof, he wondered how he'd get up there. He was a bear, not a flying reindeer. But the team immediately stepped off of it, gently floating down to land in Wyatt's front yard with the sleigh.

"Whoa." He whistled low. "Okay, Bryn. This is definitely pretty cool."

Brynna bucked in her traces with giddy excitement. "Jump in, Santa! Nick left an extra suit for you. Put it on while we're flying."

Wyatt felt like a kid again as he hopped into the sleigh and pulled on the suit Thor handed him. Then Thor gently slapped the reins over the deers' butts, earning a little ear flick and kick from Alina as they leapt into the air, sleigh and all.

The streets of Deep Hollow were very quiet in the middle of the night as they flew overhead, jingle bells whispering on the harnesses. The falling snow stayed calm and gentle, floating through the air and occasionally landing on Wyatt's face, the inside of the sleigh, and all over eight little reindeer butts. Everyone's happy, festive laughter filled the sparkling night as they soared through the skies above Deep Hollow, spreading cheer and joy and gifts to all.

Wyatt soon held the reins as Thor genially instructed him on how to do it. Brynna kept doing cute little deer bark-giggles as they flew. Beside her, Alina said in a big sister voice, "Brynna, you have to go faster. We'll never be done at this pace."

Behind them both, their mother snorted. "You both need to go faster, girls! Your father and I didn't raise slow sleigh-pullers."

Beside her, Brynna's father briefly leaned his

head over to gently touch his mate with his antlers. "No, we raised two fabulous reindeer who are both brilliant and take after their beautiful mother." At that, Brynna's mother did her own cute little bark-giggle, wiggling in the traces so the bells jingled even more.

Wyatt saw Brynna peel her lips apart in a grin that probably wasn't common to natural-born reindeer as she again called out her own happy reindeer cry into the dark. Aw, hell, yeah. This was fun. Really fun.

Best of all, he could tell Bryn was loving it. Really and truly loving doing what a reindeer shifter did on Christmas Eve. She'd been missing out on this particular holiday joy for way too long, but that didn't matter anymore.

She'd found her place here. So had Wyatt.

Together, they were home.

Kicking out at the sky, his cute mate did yet another little buck in the traces, tossing her head again and again just to hear the bells shivering with little tinkles.

"Seriously, Brynna, you're being such a newbie at this!" But Alina's tone was playful, sounding as happy as Wyatt felt.

He laughed. To his surprise, his voice sounded

deeper than usual. Huh, that was weird. But sort of neat at the same time. He tried it again.

"Ha ha ha ha!" His voice echoed into the night, drifting over the cozy houses below.

"Nah, man," Thor said. "It goes like this. Ho ho ho!" he boomed, startling Wyatt. The sound of it lingered in the sky, accompanied by the whispering bells on the sleigh as they flew through the night. "It's Christmas night magic," Thor said, flashing a grin over his white beard. "You try now."

Wyatt felt silly for maybe half a second. But all the reindeer chimed in, encouraging him. Especially Brynna, his sweet, pretty, sexy mate.

"Come on, Santa! Let's hear it," she giggled, sounding happier than he'd ever heard her.

Taking a deep breath, Wyatt did it. "Ho ho ho! HO HO HO!" he bellowed out, getting the hang of it.

"Yes!" Brynna chortled, excitedly bucking so hard that the sleigh dipped from side to side and her mother scolded her. But they were all laughing, both bear Santas and all the little reindeer.

Wyatt's heart practically burst with joy, filled with the certainty that right here in Deep Hollow was exactly where he belonged, side by side with his beautiful mate, his family, and his friends. He was home for good with Brynna by his side, celebrating the most magical time of the year.

He let pure exultation fill his voice with the joyful magic of the holiday and his wonderful life as he cried out, "HO HO HO! A Merry Christmas to all, and to all a good night!"

The End

L ips pursed, eyes slightly narrowed in critical assessment, Jessica McMillan reached forward to touch a gentle finger to the shining star on the tree. Almost holding her breath, she pushed it just the tiniest bit to the left. It snuggled perfectly into place at the very top.

There. Letting out a huge breath of relief, she turned to her friend Livy. "I think it's just right now. What do you think?"

Livy's shiny dark hair bounced on her shoulders as she nodded. "Definitely perfect. In fact, I think that's the best Christmas tree I've ever seen in my entire life. Without a doubt." She gave another decisive nod. "Absolutely."

Jessie awarded her friend a sharp look. Livy

had never been one for a good poker face. Dissolving into more giggles, she neatly side-stepped Jessie's playful swipe at her shoulder. "Don't mess with me," Jessie protested, although she let herself smile as well. "It's my first Christmas tree in my own place. Like, ever. It's a solemn moment."

With appreciable solemnity, both women regarded the two-foot-tall tree nestled into a cushion of red velvet atop the kitchen table that doubled as a writing desk and bill holder in a corner of Jessie's tiny apartment. Carefully, Jessie stepped forward to plug the small string of lights on the tree into the wall socket. With a festive little burst, they twinkled to life amidst the deliciously piney scent of the small, needled branches. She sighed with delight as Livy made admiring noises.

"See? It is perfect. I have everything I need here."

As if on cue, a slightly outraged wail punctuated her words. With the blissful rush of love that infused her every time her little angel made a noise, whether it was indecipherable baby babble, a loud burp, a rumbly fart, or even the incredibly loud screams when her sweet darling was really hungry, Jessie turned and took the three short strides to the other end of the room. Grant's chubby little legs, extending from his diapered butt, stood firmly by the low table he clung to. He futilely reached his little hands up in an apparent attempt to scale it. As Jessie reached down to pick him up, he looked at her, a small frown slicing across his brow as he once again let out an irritable string of sound, smacking one uncoordinated hand on the table leg.

Behind her, Livy said, "Wow. It's such a good thing we got you here when we did. That cute little booger is gonna be such a handful. I am so glad we were already friends, Jess. If you hadn't told me what was going on…"

Jessie, her arms now full of squirming, sweet smelling, very strong and solid little baby, turned toward her friend as she nestled her face into the top of Grant's head and breathed in his sweet baby smell. Her son. Her world.

Her own little baby *bear shifter.* Which was the Craziest. Thing. Ever.

But which also happened to be true.

Looking at Livy and her suddenly serious expression, Jessie nodded. "I can't imagine what I would've done if I hadn't known you. If you weren't from here." She waved her hand around, indicating the small, cozy little town of Deep Hollow, blanketed under snow outside her apartment. "What about the women like me out there in the world who don't have friends like you? Friends who know about, uh, shifters? What do they do, if this ever happens to them?"

Brown eyes slightly troubled, Livy stepped forward so she could cootchie-coo Grant's little belly. He loved Livy. Seeming to forget about his battle to climb the table, he giggled and smiled and shrieked up at her with joy. "That sort of situation is really rare. You and Grant were kind of the exception to the rule."

Jessie sighed. Quickly, Livy caught herself. "I'm sorry. That was insensitive." She didn't stop tickling Grant, who still giggled and squirmed, but she scrunched up her face in an apologetic expression at Jessie.

With a reassuring smile, Jessie shrugged. "It's been my reality for over a year now. Well, more like two years if you count from when I found out that I was pregnant. It's okay, Livy," she said gently to her friend, who looked genuinely contrite at having put her foot in it. "You got me *here*. I have a new family now. Seriously, who could want anything more?"

Despite the fact that she had at least a ninety percent conviction in her words, what she didn't say hung in stark relief between them.

The father of her child. That was the only thing more she could ask for. Well, that was an impossibility that was never, ever going to happen. In her experience, families didn't work. She'd accepted it, and moved on.

Mostly.

"Come on," Livy said. She brightened. "Let's get your little bundle of joy here dressed up in that cute outfit his auntie Livy got for him. Didn't she get that for him, oh, yes she did, who's the cutest little thing ever, huh?" Her voice took on the ridiculous baby voice babble adults tended to adopt around adorable little, uh, babies. "Because we have a cookie exchange to go to, don't we, little Mr. Grant baby bear cutie pie. Huh, don't we? We sure do. Even though you can't have any cookies, my sweet little boy. But your auntie Livy sure can, oh, yes, she can."

Jessie couldn't help but shake her head and smile at Livy as the two of them bundled Grant into the adorable little purple and gray snowsuit Livy had gotten him. Livy said eventually he wouldn't feel the cold nearly as much as humans did. But until he began to shift into his bear form on his own, which should be happening pretty soon since it usually started right around the time shifter kids were a year to a year and a half old, for now he still needed the warmth of as many outer layers as a human would wear. There'd been an enormous snowstorm last night, and although the roads were plowed, it was still easier to walk to Livy's sister's house, where the holiday cookie exchange was happening.

Glancing at herself in the little oval mirror she'd hung by the front door, Jessie sighed again. Well, it didn't matter that she basically looked like a disheveled new mom. It wasn't like there would be any guys at the cookie exchange, for pete's sake. Livy had said it was a girls' thing. Even if there were any men there, they sure wouldn't look twice at a woman toting around a kid. Single moms weren't exactly in vogue in the dating world.

Fifteen minutes later, they had Grant swaddled in his snowsuit, diaper bag packed, and the batch of cookies each had baked that morning tucked away into containers they took with them. The second they stepped out into the winter wonderland, Jessie couldn't help but take a deep inhale of the air, pulling the crisp cold and the deep forest scents of the Colorado winter into her. The smell was heavenly.

With Grant tucked securely against her back in the baby carrier that had been one of the many items the local bear clan—wow, did it still feel kind of funny to be thinking about things like that now —had bestowed upon her when she first came here to live in Deep Hollow with her half-shifter son, Jessie stepped through the thick drifts of snow in front of her door to the groomed sidewalk before it. "You are so lucky you grew up with this," she said to Livy, letting soft envy buff her words. "I grew up with the smell of diesel and oil and dirty big city." Just thinking about it made her wrinkle her nose slightly.

Livy laughed as they walked down the salted sidewalk. "There are plenty of reasons to leave Deep Hollow." She ticked them off on her gloved fingers. "Jobs. Men I didn't grow up with since kindergarten. Adventure. You know. The sort of opportunities you can only get in a big city."

Jessie rolled her eyes at Livy. They had diametrically opposed dreams. She knew Livy yearned for more excitement, but as far as Jessie was concerned, cities were ugly and gross and way too noisy. "I can hardly imagine moving away from this adorable little town." She shrugged. "It already feels so comfortable to me."

"Even after barely a week?" Livy teased.

Jessie nodded. "I can't really explain it," she said softly. "Deep Hollow just clicked for me. Besides, it's definitely where Grant needs to grow up." Grant cooed behind Jessie's head in the backpack carrier, one of his hands tightly catching strands of her hair that popped out from beneath her warm hat.

Livy nodded without answering. That, she understood.

A friendly silence held them the remaining block to their destination, although it was filled with Grant's endless nonsensical chatter of delight and what, Jessie decided, had to be some sort of running commentary on their surroundings. His voice warbled along in the cooing word-like noises of babies who weren't quite old enough to speak yet, but who grasped enough of language to understand they would be able to communicate that way.

As they walked, Jessie took in the holiday-filled scene of the little town, sighing with contentment. For the whole ten days she had been calling Deep Hollow her new home, she been utterly charmed by its mountain feel, the genuine friendliness of the residents, and something else she couldn't quite put her finger on.

Something that indeed felt like *home.* Even without Grant needing to grow up here, surrounded by his own bear shifter kind and taught by them, she would have loved this place. She felt more soothed here than anywhere she'd ever lived in her life. Like it had called to her.

Right now, covered in piles of billowy white snow that sparkled in the sunlight of the clear day, it was even more enticing. The old-fashioned lampposts on either side of the lone main drag as they turned down it were festooned with lights and holiday decorations. Pine trees and several of the homes on Main Street were equally decorated, along with the fronts of every single shop on the way.

Jessie hadn't known she was a mountain girl before she came here, but now she was in love with everything about it. Some of the funny town stories Livy had regaled her with let her in on some of the small, harmless secrets about the locals, making her feel even more like she belonged here. The people she was already beginning to know made her feel welcome. People like the gracious Clara who owned the post office, Lindsay the bartender/server at the local watering hole called The Tank, and Peregrine, the high school kid who was bagging groceries at the town's sole tiny grocery store full-time during his winter break to fund what he had told her with earnest excitement was a new pair of skis for his younger sister's Christmas present. Jessie knew he was a shifter. She'd yet to work up her nerve to ask how a bear shifter could be named after a bird, but she figured there was an interesting story there.

Then of course there was Maddy, Livy's sister and the owner of the bakery café where Livy had set Jessie up with a job. It didn't pay much, but it came with the apartment. Maddy was also perfectly happy for her to bring Grant to work since he was such a well-behaved baby, and everyone instantly fell in love with him.

As they strolled along Main Street, occasionally waving at people on the other side whom they knew, Jessie felt the familiar sense of amazement that just about everyone in town knew that bear shifters lived among them. Livy had told her, with a deadly earnestness that almost scared her, that in general, telling humankind about the existence of shifters just wasn't done. That was pretty obvious, since Jessie had never heard of them in her entire life. Shifters weren't nearly as common as humans in the world, Livy had confided in her. It was a given that if shifters were ever discovered, they'd be dissected to within an inch of their lives. Studied, examined, spirited away to god-awful labs where who knew what would be done to them.

Humans were pretty good at being scared of what they didn't know.

Jessie felt fierce protectiveness wash through her again at the thought of anyone ever daring to want to do such a thing to her son. Jessie had not yet witnessed him turning into a bear. But he definitely was going to. She had seen his tiny claws extending and retracting from his fingertips, dreams in which he growled in a low register that no human would naturally do. Once or twice he'd sleepily blinked his little eyes at her and she could see the shadow of his bear within them, romping around somewhere inside her son.

Seeing his little claws come out two weeks ago had been what finally sent her lunging for her phone to call Livy, almost desperately accepting her offer of a new place to live. A place where Grant could grow up among his own kind, mentored by them in how to be the bear shifter he was. True to her word, Livy and two strapping male friends of hers had hopped a plane from some local private airstrip and flown to Jessie's latest home in Minneapolis, part of her years-long hop, skip, and jump around the country trying to find a good place to settle herself. They gathered up the rather pitifully small amount of her worldly belongings, threw them all into a rental truck, which they had paid for over her strident protest, and driven everything back to Deep Hollow.

She felt a tiny shiver slip down her back as she recalled the small demonstration they'd given her right as they arrived in Deep Hollow. Just after they entered the town limits, they'd pulled over in the snowy woods off the winding little mountain road. One of the guys from the local bear clan, whom Livy had introduced as Beckett, cheerfully showed Jessie his ability to shift from his human form into an enormous grizzly bear. She'd been ready for it, since Livy had been prepping her since before Grant was even born. Even so, to see the guy be human one moment, then a giant creature the next, standing there with them as nonchalantly as any person would, had been a stunning experience.

He'd opened his giant maw and yawned with an

impressive show of gleaming sharp teeth—for which he got his shoulder smacked by Livy, who scolded him that he was going to scare Jessie.

"Wow," was all Jessie's stumbling brain had been able to come up with.

After a moment, Livy had gone to the moving truck, took Grant out of his car seat, and walked him over to the giant, humpbacked bruin. Despite herself, Jessie had stiffened and automatically reached for him, a protest rising in her throat. But before she could do or say anything, Grant stared at the giant bear, then chortled with glee and excitement as he reached out his chubby little hands. Beckett the grizzly bear had extended his nose forward very delicately, allowing Grant to feel and slap and tickle him without even moving, though he blinked his furry eyelids several times when Grant landed a fairly good one on his snout.

"Grant knows what he is, Jessie," Livy had said, throwing an understanding smile her way. "Even though he's half human, trust me. He's going to shift, and it's gonna happen really soon. It's a very good thing that he'll be around his own kind full-time," she'd quietly added.

They were safe here. Jessie again inhaled the scent of the wild, snow-covered woods as they turned down another street and up the walkway of a large Victorian style house nestled back in the trees. "Livy, this is absolutely the best gift I ever got in my life." She smiled happily as they went up the cleared walkway to the large, ornate door of Maddy's house. "I finally feel like I can relax."

Livy smiled. "I'm so glad, Jessie." She gently chucked Grant under his chin, the dopey smile that everyone in town seemed to get every time they looked at him coming across her face as he uttered his usual cute little baby coos and gurgles at her. "You deserve some stability and quiet after everything you've been through."

"I sure do." Jessie sighed with contentment as Livy knocked on the door.

Almost instantly, it opened, sending out a whoosh of warmth, the happy chatter and laughter of many voices inside, the delicious scents of baking cookies.

And a deeper, darker, far more intense something else beneath it all.

A *something* that swept through Jessie like a delicious, icy wind of alertness and clarity. A touch musky, yet crisp like snow, wild and rough, the scent slammed through her with an intensity she'd never before experienced.

"Hey, Shane," Livy said in oblivious cheer as she pulled off her scarf and hat, stepping toward the door. "I thought you were still out of town. Did the big ole manly grizzly bear come back just for our girly cookie exchange?" she teased. Then she gestured at Jessie. "This is Jessie, she's new here. Jessie, meet Shane, another one of our resident hulking shifters."

Jessie stood rooted in front of the door, staring at the enormous guy filling the entire frame. Her jaw dropped as her eyes slowly traveled upward to find his. The guy was massive. Just like all the other male bear shifters she'd met so far, but he seemed even bigger. He must be 6'5", she thought to herself in a daze. A half-wild tousle of golden brown hair on top of his head was at odds with the darker, neatly trimmed beard and mustache that bristled out from his granite hard, drop-dead gorgeous face. Light whiskey eyes that seemed familiar looked back at Jessie with as much startlement, his strong lips somewhat parted and sending the bizarre image of absolutely ravaging her with kisses as Jessie stared back at him, completely frozen.

Whoa, she thought, still dazed, *he's a freaking sexy as hell bear shifter lumberjack god of the woods.*

Except lumberjacks had never looked this sexy, she was pretty sure. Especially—

Especially ones she recognized.

Wait a minute.

Holy.

Freaking.

Nuh-uh.

He looked like—

"Maverick?" Jessie's voice was strangled as the name she had often thought about for the past two years managed to shove its way out of her mouth. She sensed more than saw Livy's smile falter as her head suddenly swiveled back and forth between Jessie and Mr. sexy lumberjack bear shifter dude. "You have a beard now," she whispered stupidly.

His own voice rumbling out so deeply it vibrated through her body, he replied in an equally shocked tone, "Jessie? What—what the hell are you doing here?"

Grant chose that moment to emit one of the screeching little kid cries of those not quite into toddlerhood, demanding the attention come back to him. Obligingly, three sets of eyes clamped on him, though all Jessie could see was the corner of his face since he was still ensconced in the backpack carrier. He waved his snow-suited arms around, almost seeming to reach forward to Mav.

"Who—what—no, no, no. That's *Shane*," Livy stuttered, eyes about popping out of her head. "He's the handyman up at the lodge. You said the guy's name was Maverick. And that he was some sort of fighter dude on the underground rings." Her wide eyes darted between them. "No way."

Seeing Jessie's expression, then that of the sexy guy Jessie knew as Maverick, Livy's face slackened. "Oh, my god," she breathed. She looked from Grant to Jessie, then back to Grant. Then she gestured at the huge, gorgeous man taking up all the space in the doorway. "No freaking way. This is him? For real? *He's* your baby daddy? Shane Walker from Deep Hollow is Grant's father?" Her voice dropped to a stunned whisper.

Jessie shook her head, completely lost as she stared into the achingly familiar face of the man she'd been looking for ever since she found out she was pregnant.

The man with whom she'd spent the most erotic, blissful, exciting three days of her entire life.

The man who was the father of her bear shifter son.

Christmas Night Bear: Wyatt (Wyatt & Brynna)

ABOUT J.K.

J.K. Harper lives in the rugged, gorgeous canyon country of the southwest, which is a great place to let her imagination run wild.

For more information about her books, please visit her website: www.jkharper.com.

ALSO BY J.K. HARPER

Silvertip Shifters
Hunter's Moon: Quentin (*Black Mesa Wolves crossover*)
Mountain Bear's Baby: Shane
Taming Her Bear: Beckett
Rescue Bear: Cortez
Ranger Bear: Riley
Firefighter Bear: Slade
Superstar Bear: Bodhi
Christmas Night Bear: Wyatt

Black Mesa Wolves
Guardian Wolf
Alpha Wolf
Hunting Wolf

Wild Wolf

Solstice Wolf

Christmas Wolf

New Year Wolf

Protector Wolf

Fire Wolf

Rogue Wolf

Dragon Mates

Dazzled

Thrilled

Burned

Wicked Wolf Shifters

Surrendered to the Pack: Volume 1, Episode 1

Claimed by the Pack: Volume 1, Episode 2

Taken by the Pack: Volume 1, Episode 3

Mated to the Pack: Volume 1, Episode 4

Wicked Wolf Shifters: Complete Volume 1

Ruled by the Pack: Volume 2, Episode 1

Hunted by the Pack: Volume 2, Episode 2

Destined for the Pack: Volume 2, Episode 3

Wicked Wolf Shifters: Complete Volume 2

Made in the USA
Lexington, KY
30 November 2019